Carry On

Coningsby Dawson

Contents

CARRY ON

BY

Coningsby Dawson

WHEN THE WAR'S AT AN END

At length when the war's at an end
And we're just ourselves,--you and I,
And we gather our lives up to mend,
We, who've learned how to live and to die:

Shall we think of the old ambition
For riches, or how to grow wise,
When, like Lazarus freshly arisen,
We've the presence of Death in our eyes?

Shall we dream of our old life's passion,--
To toil for our heart's desire,
Whose souls War has taken to fashion
With molten death and with fire?

I think we shall crave the laughter
Of the wind through trees gold with the sun,
When our strife is all finished,--after
The carnage of War is done.

Just these things will then seem worth while:--
How to make Life more wondrously sweet;
How to live with a song and a smile,
How to lay our lives at Love's feet.

                              ERIC P. DAWSON,

INTRODUCTION

The letters in this volume were not written for publication. They are intimate and personal in a high degree. They would not now be published by those to whom they are addressed, had they not come to feel that the spirit and temper of the writer might do something to strengthen and invigorate those who, like himself, are called on to make great sacrifices for high causes and solemn duties.

They do not profess to give any new information about the military operations of the Allies; this is the task of the publicist, and at all times is forbidden to the soldier in the field. Here and there some striking or significant fact has been allowed to pass the censor; but the value of the letters does not lie in these things. It is found rather in the record of how the dreadful yet heroic realities of war affect an unusually sensitive mind, long trained in moral and romantic idealism; the process by which this mind adapts itself to unanticipated and incredible conditions, to acts and duties which lie close to horror, and are only saved from being horrible by the efficacy of the spiritual effort which they evoke. Hating the brutalities of War, clearly perceiving the wide range of its cruelties, yet the heart of the writer is never hardened by its daily commerce with death; it is purified by pity and terror, by heroism and sacrifice, until the whole nature seems fresh annealed into a finer strength.

The intimate nature of these letters makes it necessary to say something about the writer.

Coningsby Dawson graduated with honours in history from Oxford in 1905, and in the same year came to the United States with the intention of taking a theological course at Union Seminary. After a year at the Seminary he reached the conclusion that his true lifework lay in literature, and he at once began to fit himself for his vocation. In the meantime his family left England, and we had made our home in Taunton, Massachusetts. Here, in a quiet house, amid lawns and leafy elms, he gave himself with indefatigable ardour to the art of writing. He wrote from seven to ten hours a day, producing many poems, short stories, and three novels. Few writers have ever worked harder to attain literary excellence, or have practised a more austere devotion to their art. I often marvelled how a young man, fresh from a brilliant career at the greatest of English Universities, could be content with a life that was so widely separated from association with men and affairs. I wondered still more at the patience with which he endured the rebuffs that always await the beginner in literature, and the humility with which he was willing to learn the hard lessons of his apprenticeship in literary form. The secret lay, no doubt, in his secure sense of a vocation, and his belief that good work could not fail in the end to justify itself. But, not the less, these four years of obscure drudgery wore upon his spirit, and hence some of the references in these letters to his days of self-despising. The period of waiting came to an end at last with the publication in 1913 of his **Garden Without Walls**, which attained immediate success. When he speaks in these letters of his brief burst of fame, he refers to those crowded months in the Fall of 1913, when his novel was being discussed on every hand, and, for the first time, he met many writers of established reputation as an equal.

Another novel, **The Raft**, followed **The Garden Without Walls**. The nature of his life now seemed fixed. To the task of novel-writing he had brought a temperament highly idealistic and romantic, a fresh and vivid imagination, and a thorough literary equipment. His life, as he planned it, held but one purpose for him, outside the warmth and tenacity of its affections--the triumph of the efficient purpose in the adequate expression of his mind in literature. The austerity of his long years of preparation had left him relatively indifferent to the common prizes of life, though they had done nothing to lessen his intense joy in life. His whole mind was concentrated on his art. His adventures would be the adventures of the mind in search of ampler modes of expression. His crusades would be the crusades of the spirit in search of the realities of truth. He had received the public recognition which gave him faith in himself and faith in his ability to achieve the reputation of the true artist, whose work is not cheapened but dignified and broadened by success. So he read the future, and so his critics read it for him. And then, sudden and unheralded, there broke on this quiet life of intellectual devotion the great storm of 1914. The guns that roared along the Marne shattered all his purposes, and left him face to face with a solemn spiritual exigency which admitted no equivocation.

At first, in common with multitudes more experienced than himself, he did not fully comprehend the true measure of the cataclysm which had overwhelmed the world. There had been wars before, and they had been fought out by standing armies. It was incredible that any war should last more than a few months. Again and again the world had been assured that war would break down with its own weight, that no war could be financed beyond a certain brief period, that the very nature of modern warfare, with its terrible engines of destruction, made swift decisions a necessity. The conception of a British War which involved the entire manhood of the nation was new, and unparalleled in past history. And the further conception of a war so vast in its issues that it really threatened the very existence of the nation was new too. Alarmists had sometimes predicted these things, but they had been disbelieved. Historians had used such phrases of long past struggles, but often as a mode of rhetoric rather than as the expression of exact truth. Yet, in a very few weeks, it became evident that not alone England, but the entire fabric of liberal civilisation was threatened by a power that knew no honour, no restraints of either caution or magnanimity, no ethic but the armed might that trampled under blood-stained feet all the things which the common sanction of centuries held dearest and fairest.

Perhaps, if Coningsby had been resident in England, these realities of the situation would have been immediately apparent. Residing in America, the real outlines of the struggle were a little dimmed by distance. Nevertheless, from the very first he saw clearly where his duty lay. He could not enlist immediately. He was bound in honour to fulfil various literary obligations. His latest book, **Slaves of Freedom**, was in process of being adapted for serial use, and its publication would follow. He set the completion of this work as the period when he must enlist; working on with difficult self-restraint toward the appointed hour. If he had regrets for a career broken at the very point where it had reached success and was assured of more than competence, he never expressed them. His one regret was the effect of his enlistment on those most closely bound to him by affections which had been deepened and made more tender by the sense of common exile. At last the hour came when he was free to follow the imperative call of patriotic duty. He went to Ottawa, saw

Sir Sam Hughes, and was offered a commission in the Canadian Field Artillery on the completion of his training at the Royal Military College, at Kingston, Ontario. The last weeks of his training were passed at the military camp of Petewawa on the Ottawa River. There his family was able to meet him in the July of 1916. While we were with him he was selected, with twenty-four other officers, for immediate service in France; and at the same time his two younger brothers enlisted in the Naval Patrol, then being recruited in Canada by Commander Armstrong.

The letters in this volume commence with his departure from Ottawa. Week by week they have come, with occasional interruptions; mud stained epistles, written in pencil, in dug-outs by the light of a single candle, in the brief moments snatched from hard and perilous duties. They give no hint of where he was on the far-flung battle-line. We know now that he was at Albert, at Thiepval, at Courcelette, and at the taking of the Regina trench, where, unknown to him, one of his cousins fell in the heroic charge of the Canadian infantry. His constant thoughtfulness for those who were left at home is manifest in all he writes. It has been expressed also in other ways, dear and precious to remember: in flowers delivered by his order from the battlefield each Sabbath morning at our house in Newark, in cables of birthday congratulations, which arrived on the exact date. Nothing has been forgotten that could alleviate the loneliness of our separation, or stimulate our courage, or make us conscious of the unbroken bond of love.

The general point of view in these letters is, I think, adequately expressed in the phrase "Carry On," which I have used as the title of this book. It was our happy lot to meet Coningsby in London in the January of the present year, when he was granted ten days' leave. In the course of conversation one night he laid emphasis on the fact that he, and those who served with him, were, after all, not professional soldiers, but civilians at war. They did not love war, and when the war was ended not five per cent of them would remain in the army. They were men who had left professions and vocations which still engaged the best parts of their minds, and would return to them when the hour came. War was for them an occupation, not a vocation. Yet they had proved themselves, one and all, splendid soldiers, bearing the greatest hardships without complaint, and facing wounds and death with a gay courage which had made the Canadian forces famous even among a host of men, equally brave and heroic. The secret of their fortitude lay in the one brief phrase,

"Carry On." Their fortitude was of the spirit rather than the nerves. They were aware of the solemn ideals of justice, liberty, and righteousness for which they fought, and would never give up till they were won. In the completeness of their surrender to a great cause they had been lifted out of themselves to a new plane of living by the transformation of their spirit. It was the dogged indomitable drive of spiritual forces controlling bodily forces. Living or dying those forces would prevail. They would carry on to the end, however long the war, and would count no sacrifice too great to assure its triumph.

This is the spirit which breathes through these letters. The splendour of war, as my son puts it, is in nothing external; it is all in the souls of the men. "There's a marvellous grandeur about all this carnage and desolation--men's souls rise above the distress--they have to, in order to survive." "Every man I have met out here has the amazing guts to wear his crown of thorns as though it were a cap-and-bells." They have shredded off their weaknesses, and attained that "corporate stout-heartedness" which is "the acme of what Aristotle meant by virtue." For himself, he discovers that the plague of his former modes of life lay in self-distrust. It was the disease of the age. The doubt of many things which it were wisdom to believe had ended in the doubt of one's own capacity for heroism. All those doubts and self-despisings had vanished in the supreme surrender to sacrificial duty. The doors of the Kingdom of Heroism were flung so wide that the meanest might enter in, and in that act the humblest became comrades of Drake's men, who could jest as they died. No one knows his real strength till it is put to the test; the highest joy of life is to discover that the soul can meet the test, and survive it.

The Somme battlefield, from which all these letters were despatched, is an Inferno much more terrible than any Dante pictured. It is a vast sea of mud, full of the unburied dead, pitted and pock-marked by shell-holes, treeless and horseless, "the abomination of desolation." And the men who toil across it look more like outcasts of the London Embankment than soldiers. "They're loaded down like pack-animals, their shoulders are rounded, they're wearied to death, but they go on and go on.... There's no flash of sword or splendour of uniforms. They're only very tired men determined to carry on. The war will be won by tired men who can never again pass an insurance test." Yet they carry on--the "broken counter-jumper, the ragged ex-plumber," the clerk from the office, the man from the farm; Londoner, Canadian,

Australian, New Zealander, men drawn from every quarter of the Empire, who daily justify their manhood by devotion to an ideal and by contempt of death. And in the heart of each there is a settled conviction that the cause for which they have sacrificed so much must triumph. They have no illusions about an early peace. They see their comrades fall, and say quietly, "He's gone West." They do heroic things daily, which in a lesser war would have won the Victoria Cross, but in this war are commonplaces. They know themselves re-born in soul, and are dimly aware that the world is travailing toward new birth with them. They are still very human, men who end their letters with a row of crosses which stand for kisses. They are not de-humanised by war; the kindliness and tenderness of their natures are unspoiled by all their daily traffic in horror. But they have won their souls; and when the days of peace return these men will take with them to the civilian life a tonic strength and nobleness which will arrest and extirpate the decadence of society with the saving salt of valour and of faith.

It may be said also that they do not hate their foe, although they hate the things for which he fights. They are fighting a clean fight, with men whose courage they respect. A German prisoner who comes into the British camp is sure of good treatment. He is neither starved nor insulted. His captors share with him cheerfully their rations and their little luxuries. Sometimes a sullen brute will spit in the face of his captor when he offers him a cigarette; he is always an officer, never a private. And occasionally between these fighting hosts there are acts of magnanimity which stand out illumined against the dark background of death and suffering. One of the stories told me by my son illustrates this. During one fierce engagement a British officer saw a German officer impaled on the barbed wire, writhing in anguish. The fire was dreadful, yet he still hung there unscathed. At length the British officer could stand it no longer. He said quietly, "I can't bear to look at that poor chap any longer." So he went out under the hail of shell, released him, took him on his shoulders and carried him to the German trench. The firing ceased. Both sides watched the act with wonder. Then the Commander in the German trench came forward, took from his own bosom the Iron Cross, and pinned it on the breast of the British officer. Such an episode is true to the holiest ideals of chivalry; and it is all the more welcome because the German record is stained by so many acts of barbarism, which the world cannot forgive.

This magnanimous attitude toward the enemy is very apparent in these letters. The man whose mind is filled with great ideals of sacrifice and duty has no room for the narrowness of hate. He can pity a foe whose sufferings exceed his own, and the more so because he knows that his foe is doomed. The British troops do know this to-day by many infallible signs. In the early days of the war untrained men, poorly equipped with guns, were pitted against the best trained troops in Europe. The first Canadian armies were sacrificed, as was that immortal army of Imperial troops who saved the day at Mons. The Canadians often perished in that early fighting by the excess of their own reckless bravery. They are still the most daring fighters in the British army, but they have profited by the hard discipline of the past. They know now that they have not only the will to conquer, but the means of conquest. Their, artillery has become conspicuous for its efficiency. It is the ceaseless artillery fire which has turned the issue of the war for the British forces. The work of the infantry is beyond praise. They "go over the top" with superb courage, and all who have seen them are ready to say with my son, "I'm hats off to the infantry." And in this final efficiency, surpassing all that could have been thought possible in the earlier stages of the war, the British forces read the clear augury of victory. The war will be won by the Allied armies; not only because they fight for the better cause, which counts for much, in spite of Napoleon's cynical saying that "God is on the side of the strongest battalions"; but because at last they have superiority in equipment, discipline and efficiency. Upon that shell-torn Western front, amid the mud and carnage of the Somme, there has been slowly forged the weapon which will drive the Teuton enemy across the Rhine, and give back to Europe and the world unhindered liberty and enduring peace.

W.J. DAWSON.
March, 1917.

THE LETTERS

In order to make some of the allusions in these letters clear I will set down briefly the circumstances which explain them, and supply a narrative link where it may be required.

I have already mentioned the Military Camp at Petewawa, on the Ottawa river. The Camp is situated about seven miles from Pembroke. The Ottawa river is at this point a beautiful lake. Immediately opposite the Camp is a little summer hotel of the simplest description. It was at this hotel that my wife, my daughter, and myself stayed in the early days of July, 1916.

The hotel was full of the wives of the officers stationed in the Camp. During the daytime I was the only man among the guests. About five o'clock in the afternoon the officers from the Camp began to arrive on a primitive motor ferryboat. My son came over each day, and we often visited him at the Camp. His long training at Kingston had been very severe. It included besides the various classes which he attended a great deal of hard exercise, long rides or foot marches over frozen roads before breakfast, and so forth. After this strenuous winter the Camp at Petewawa was a delightful change. His tent stood on a bluff, commanding an exquisite view of the broad stretch of water, diversified by many small islands. We had a great deal of swimming in the lake, and several motor-boat excursions to its beautiful upper reaches. One afternoon when we went over in our launch to meet him at the Camp wharf, he told us that that day a General had come from Ottawa to ask for twenty-five picked officers to supply the casualties among the Canadian Field Artillery at the front. He had immediately volunteered and been accepted.

At this time my two younger sons, who had joined us at Petewawa in order to see their brother, enrolled themselves in the Royal Naval Motor Patrol Service, and had to return to Nelson, British Columbia, to settle their affairs. Near Nelson, on the

Kootenay Lake, we have a large fruit ranch, managed by my second son, Reginald. My youngest son, Eric, was with a law-firm in Nelson, and had just passed his final examinations as solicitor and barrister.

This ranch had played a great part in our lives. The scenery is among the finest in British Columbia. We usually spent our summers there, finding not only continual interest in the development of our orchards, but a great deal of pleasure in riding, swimming, and boating. We had often talked of building a modern house there, but had never done so. The original "little shack" was the work of Reginald's own hands, in the days when most of the ranch was primeval forest. It had been added to, but was still of the simplest description. One reason why we had not built a modern house was that this "little shack" had become much endeared to us by association and memory. We were all together there more than once, and Coningsby had written a great deal there. We built later on a sort of summer library--a big room on the edge of a beautiful ravine--to which reference is made in later letters. Some of the happiest days of our lives were spent in these lovely surroundings, and the memory of those blue summer days, amid the fragrance of miles of pine-forest, often recurs to Coningsby as he writes from the mud-wastes of the Somme.

We left Petewawa to go to the ranch before Coningsby sailed for England, that we might get our other two sons ready for their journey to England. They left us on August 21st, and the ranch was sub-let to Chinamen in the end of September, when we returned to Newark, New Jersey.

CARRY ON

I

OTTAWA, July 16th, 1916.
DEAREST ALL:

So much has happened since last I saw you that it's difficult to know where to start. On Thursday, after lunch, I got the news that we were to entrain from Petewawa next Friday morning. I at once put in for leave to go to Ottawa the next day until the following Thursday at reveille. We came here with a lot of the other officers who are going over and have been having a very full time.

I am sailing from a port unknown on board the *Olympic* with 6,000 troops--there is to be a big convoy. I feel more than ever I did--and I'm sure it's a feeling that you share since visiting the camp--that I am setting out on a Crusade from which it would have been impossible to withhold myself with honour. I go quite gladly and contentedly, and pray that in God's good time we may all sit again in the little shack at Kootenay and listen to the rustling of the orchard outside. It will be of those summer days that I shall be thinking all the time.

Yours, with very much love,

CON.

II

HALIFAX, July 23rd.

MY DEAR ONES:

We've spent all morning on the dock, seeing to our baggage, and have just got leave ashore for two hours. We have had letters handed to us saying that on no account are we to mention anything concerning our passage overseas, neither are we allowed to cable our arrival from the other side until four clear days have elapsed.

You are thinking of me this quiet Sunday morning at the ranch, and I of you. And I am wishing--As I wish, I stop and ask myself, "Would I be there if I could have my choice?" And I remember those lines of Emerson's which you quoted:

"Though love repine and reason chafe,
There comes a voice without reply,
'Twere man's perdition to be safe,
When for the Truth he ought to die."

I wouldn't turn back if I could, but my heart cries out against "the voice which speaks without reply."

Things are growing deeper with me in all sorts of ways. Family affections stand out so desirably and vivid, like meadows green after rain. And religion means more. The love of a few dear human people and the love of the divine people out of sight, are all that one has to lean on in the graver hours of life. I hope I come back again--I very much hope I come back again; there are so many finer things that I could do with the rest of my days--bigger things. But if by any chance I should cross the seas to stay, you'll know that that also will be right and as big as anything that I could do with life, and something that you'll be able to be just as proud about as if I had lived to fulfil all your other dear hopes for me. I don't suppose I shall talk of this again. But I wanted you to know that underneath all the lightness and ambition there's something that I learnt years ago in Highbury[1]. I've become a little child again in God's hands, with full confidence in His love and wisdom, and a growing trust that whatever He decides for me will be best and kindest.

[Footnote 1: We resided over thirteen years at Highbury, London, N., during my pastorate of the Highbury Quadrant Congregational Church.]

This is the last letter I shall be able to send to you before the other boys follow me. Keep brave, dear ones, for all our sakes; don't let any of us turn cowards whatever ultimately happens. We've a tradition to live up to now that we have become a family of soldiers and sailors.

I shall long for the time when you come over to England. Where will our meeting be and when? Perhaps the war may be ended and then won't you be glad that we dared all this sorrow of good-byes?

God bless and keep you,
CON.

III

ON BOARD, July 27th, 1916.
My VERY DEAR PEOPLE:
Here we are scooting along across the same old Atlantic we've crossed so many times on journeys of pleasure. I'm at a loss to make my letters interesting, as we are allowed to say little concerning the voyage and everything is censored.

There are men on board who are going back to the trenches for the second time. One of them is a captain in the Princess Pat's, who is badly scarred in his neck and cheek and thighs, and has been in Canada recuperating. There is also a young flying chap who has also seen service. They are all such boys and so plucky in the face of certain knowledge.

This morning I woke up thinking of our motor-tour of two years ago in England, and especially of our first evening at The Three Cups in Dorset. I feel like running down there to see it all again if I get any leave on landing. How strange it will be to go back to Highbury again like this! The little boy who ran back and forth to school down Paradise Row little thought of the person who to-day masquerades as his elder self.

Heigho! I wish I could tell you a lot of things that I'm not allowed to. This letter would be much more interesting then.

In seventeen days the boys will also have left you--so this will arrive when you're horribly lonely. I'm so sorry for you dear people--but I'd be sorrier for you if we were all with you. If I were a father or mother, I'd rather have my sons dead than see them failing when the supreme sacrifice was called for. I marvel all the time at the prosaic and even coarse types of men who have risen to the greatness of the occasion. And there's not a man aboard who would have chosen the job ahead of him. One man here used to pay other people to kill his pigs because he couldn't endure the cruelty of doing it himself. And now he's going to kill men. And he's a sample. I wonder if there is a Lord God of Battles--or is he only an invention of man and an excuse for man's own actions.

Monday.

We are just in--safely arrived in spite of everything. I hope you had no scare reports of our having been sunk--such reports often get about when a big troop ship is on the way.

I'm baggage master for my draft, and have to get on deck now. You'll have a long letter from me soon.

Good-bye,
Yours ever,
Con.

IV

SHORNCLIFF, August 19th, 1916.

MY DEAREST:

We haven't had any hint of what is going to happen to us--whether Field Artillery, the Heavies or trench mortars. There seems little doubt that we are to be in England for a little while taking special courses.

I read father's letter yesterday. You are very brave--you never thought that you would be the father of a soldier and sailors; and, as you say, there's a kind of tradition about the way in which the fathers of soldiers and sailors should act. Confess--aren't you more honestly happy to be our father as we are now than as we were? I know quite well you are, in spite of the loneliness and heartache. We've all been forced into a heroism of which we did not think ourselves capable. We've been carried up to the Calvary of the world where it is expedient that a few men should suffer that all the generations to come may be better.

I understand in a dim way all that you suffer--the sudden divorce of all that we had hoped for from the present--the ceaseless questionings as to what lies ahead. Your end of the business is the worse. For me, I can go forward steadily because of the greatness of the glory. I never thought to have the chance to suffer in my body for other men. The insufficiency of merely setting nobilities down on paper is finished. How unreal I seem to myself! Can it be true that I am here and you are in the still aloofness of the Rockies? I think the multitude of my changes has blunted my perceptions. I trudge along like a traveller between high hedgerows; my heart is blinkered so that I am scarcely aware of landscapes. My thoughts are always with you--I make calculations for the differences of time that I may follow more accurately your doings. I'd love to come down to the study summer-house and watch the blueness of the lake with you--I love those scenes and memories more than any in the world.

Good-bye for the present. Be brave.

Yours,
Con.

V

SHORNCLIFF, August 19th, 1916.
MY DEARS:
It's not quite three weeks to-day since I came to England, and it seems ages.
The first week was spent on leave, the second I passed my exams in gun drill and
gun-laying, and this week I have finished my riding. Next Monday I start on my
gunnery.

Do you remember Captain S. at the Camp? I had his young brother to dinner
with me last night-he's just back from France minus an eye. He lasted three and a
half weeks, and was buried four feet deep by a shell. He's a jolly boy, as cheerful as
you could want and is very good company. He gave me a vivid description. He had
a great boy-friend. At the start of the war they both joined, S. in the Artillery, his
friend in the Mounted Rifles. At parting they exchanged identification tokens. S.'s
bore his initials and the one word "Violets"--which meant that they were his favourite flower and he would like to have some scattered over him when he was buried.
His friend wore his initials and the words "No flowers by request." It was S.'s first
week out--they were advancing, having driven back the enemy, and were taking
up a covered position in a wood from which to renew their offensive. It was night,
black as pitch, but they knew that the wood must have been the scene of fighting
by the scuttling of the rats. Suddenly the moon came out, and from beneath a bush
S. saw a face--or rather half a face--which he thought he recognised, gazing up at
him. He corrects himself when he tells the story, and says that it wasn't so much
the disfigured features as the profile that struck him as familiar. He bent down and
searched beneath the shirt, and drew out a little metal disc with "No flowers by
request" written on it.

I don't know whether I ought to repeat things like that to you, but the description was so graphic. I have met many who have returned from the Front, and what

puzzles me in all of them is their unawed acceptance of death. I don't think I could ever accept it as natural; it's too discourteous in its interruption of many dreams and plans and loves.

Yours with very much love,
Con.

VI

SHORNCLIFF, August 30th, 1916.
MY DEARESTS:

I have just returned from sending you a cable to let you know that I'm off to France. The word came out in orders yesterday, and I shall leave before the end of the week with a draft of officers--I have been in England just a day over four weeks. My only regret is that I shall miss the boys who should be travelling up to London about the same time as I am setting out for the Front. After I have been there for three months I am supposed to get a leave--this should be due to me about the beginning of December, and you can judge how I shall count on it. Think of the meeting with R. and E., and the immensity of the joy.

Selfishly I wish that you were here at this moment--actually I'm glad that you are away. Everybody goes out quite unemotionally and with very few good-byes--we made far more fuss in the old days about a week-end visit.

Now that at last it has come--this privileged moment for which I have worked and waited--my heart is very quiet. It's the test of a character which I have often doubted. I shall be glad not to have to doubt it again. Whatever happens, I know you will be glad to remember that at a great crisis I tried to play the man, however small my qualifications. We have always lived so near to one another's affections that this going out alone is more lonely to me than to most men. I have always had some one near at hand with love-blinded eyes to see my faults as springing from higher motives. Now I reach out my hands across six thousand miles and only touch yours with my imagination to say good-bye. What queer sights these eyes, which have been almost your eyes, will witness! If my hands do anything respectable, re-member that it is your hands that are doing it. It is your influence as a family that has made me ready for the part I have to play, and where I go, you follow me.

Poor little circle of three loving persons, please be tremendously brave. Don't let anything turn you into cowards--we've all got to be worthy of each other's sac-rifice; the greater the sacrifice may prove to be for the one the greater the nobility demanded of the remainder. How idle the words sound, and yet they will take deep meanings when time has given them graver sanctions. I think gallant is the word I've been trying to find--we must be gallant English women and gentlemen.

It's been raining all day and I got very wet this morning. Don't you wish I had caught some quite harmless sickness? When I didn't want to go back to school, I used to wet my socks purposely in order to catch cold, but the cold always avoid-ed me when I wanted it badly. How far away the childish past seems--almost as though it never happened. And was I really the budding novelist in New York? Life has become so stern and scarlet--and so brave. From my window I look out on the English Channel, a cold, grey-green sea, with rain driving across it and a fleet of small craft taking shelter. Over there beyond the curtain of mist lies France--and everything that awaits me.

News has just come that I have to start. Will continue from France.

Yours ever lovingly,
Con.

VII

Friday, September 1st, 1916, 11 am.
DEAREST FATHER AND MOTHER:
I embark at 12.30--so this is the last line before I reach France. I expect the boys are now within sight of English shores--I wish I could have had an hour with them.

I'm going to do my best to bring you honour--remember that--I shall do things for your sake out there, living up to the standards you have taught me.

Yours with a heart full of love,
Con.

VIII

FRANCE, September 1st, 1916.
DEAREST M.:
Here I am in France with the same strange smells and street cries, and almost the same little boys bowling hoops over the very cobbly cobble stones. I had afternoon tea at a patisserie and ate a great many gateaux for the sake of old times. We had a very choppy crossing, and you would most certainly have been sick had you been on board. It seemed to me that I must be coming on one of those romantic holidays to see churches and dead history--only the khaki-clad figures reminded me that I was coming to see history in the making. It's a funny world that batters us about so. It's three years since I was in France--the last time was with Arthur in Provence. It's five years since you and I did our famous trip together.

I wish you were here--there are heaps of English nurses in the streets. I expect to sleep in this place and proceed to my destination to-morrow. How I wish I could send you a really descriptive letter! If I did, I fear you would not get it--so I have to write in generalities. None of this seems real--it's a kind of wild pretence from which I shall awake-and when I tell you my dream you'll laugh and say, "How absurd of you, dreaming that you were a soldier. I must say you look like it."

Good-bye, my dearest girl,
God bless you,
Con.

IX

September 8th, 1916.

MY DEAREST ONES:

I'm sending this to meet you on your return from Kootenay. I left England on September 1st and had a night at my point of disembarkation, and then set off on a wandering adventure in search of my division. I'm sure you'll understand that I cannot enter into any details--I can only give you general and purely personal impressions. There were two other officers with me, both from Montreal. We had to picnic on chocolate and wine for twenty-four hours through our lack of forethought in not supplying ourselves with food for the trip. I shaved the first morning with water from the exhaust of a railroad engine, having first balanced my mirror on the step. The engineer was fascinated with my safety razor. There were Tommies from the trenches in another train, muddied to the eyes--who showed themselves much more resourceful. They cooked themselves quite admirable meals as they squatted on the rails, over little fires on which they perched tomato cans. Sunday evening we saw our first German prisoners--a young and degenerate-looking lot. Sunday evening we got off at a station in the rain, and shouldered our own luggage. Our luggage, by the way, consists of a sleeping bag, in which much of our stuff is packed, and a kit sack--for an immediate change and toilet articles one carries a haversack hung across the shoulder. Well, as I say, we alighted and coaxed a military wagon to come to our rescue. As we set off through a drizzling rain, trudging behind the cart, a double rainbow shone, which I took for an omen. Presently we came to a rest camp, where we told our sad story of empty tummies, and were put up for the night. A Jock--all Highlanders are called Jock--looked after us. Next morning we started out afresh in a motor lorry and finished at a Y.M.C.A. tent, where we stayed two nights. On Wednesday we met the General in Command of our Division, who posted me to the battery, which is said to be the best in the best brigade in the best division--so you may see I'm in luck. I found the battery just having come out of action--we expect to go back again in a day or two. Major B. is the O.C.--a fine man. The lieutenant who shares my tent won the Military Cross at Ypres last Spring.

I'm very happy--which will make you happy--and longing for my first taste of real war.

How strangely far away I am from you--all the experiences so unshared and different. Long before this reaches you I shall have been in action several times. This time three years ago my streak of luck came to me and I was prancing round New York. To-day I am much more genuinely happy in mind, for I feel, as I never felt when I was only writing, that I am doing something difficult which has no element of self in it. If I come back, life will be a much less restless affair.

This letter! I can imagine it being delivered and the shout from whoever takes it and the comments. I make the contrast in my mind--this little lean-to spread of canvas about four feet high, the horse-lines, guns, sentries going up and down--and then the dear home and the well-loved faces.

Good-bye. Don't be at all nervous.
Yours lovingly,
Con.

X

September 12th, Tuesday.
DEAREST M.:
You will already have received my first letters giving you my address over here. The wagon has just come up to our position, but it has brought me only one letter since I've been across. I'm sitting in my dug-out with shells passing over my head with the sound of ripping linen. I've already had the novel experience of firing a battery, and to-morrow I go up to the first line trenches.

It's extraordinary how commonplace war becomes to a man who is thrust among others who consider it commonplace. Not fifty yards away from me a dead German lies rotting and uncovered--I daresay he was buried once and then blown out by a shell.

Wednesday, 7 p.m.

Your letters came two hours ago--the first to reach me here--and I have done little else but read and re-read them. How they bring the old ways of life back with their love and longing! Dear mother's tie will be worn to-morrow, and it will be ripping to feel that it was made by her hands. Your cross has not arrived yet, dear. Your mittens will be jolly for the winter. I've heard nothing from the boys yet.

To-day I took a trip into No-Man's Land--when the war is ended I'll be able to tell you all about it. I think the picture is photographed upon my memory forever. There's so much you would like to hear and so little I'm allowed to tell. Ask G.M.'C. if he was at Princeton with a man named Price--an instructor there.

You ought to see the excitement when the water-cart brings us our mail and the letters are handed out. Some of the gunners have evidently told their Canadian girls that they are officers, and so they are addressed on their letters as lieutenants. I have to censor some of their replies, and I can tell you they are as often funny as pathetic. The ones to their mothers are childish, too, and have rows of kisses. I think men are always kiddies if you look beneath the surface. The snapshots did fill me with a wanting to be with you in Kootenay. But that's not where you'll receive this. There'll probably be a fire in the sitting-room at home, and a strong aroma of coffee and tobacco. You'll be sitting in a low chair before the fire and your fingers rubbing the hair above your left ear as you read this aloud. I'd like to walk in on you and say, "No more need for letters now." Some day soon, I pray and expect.

Tell dear Papa and Mother that their answers come next. What a lot of love you each one manage to put into your written pages! I'm afraid if I let myself go that way I might make you unhappy.

Since writing this far I have had supper. I'm now sleeping in a new dug-out and get a shower of mould on my sleeping-kit each time the guns are fired. One doesn't mind that particularly, especially when you know that the earth walls make you safe. I have a candle in an old petrol tin and dodge the shadows as I write. You know, this artillery game is good sport and one takes everything as it comes with a joke. The men are splendid--their cheeriness comes up bubbling whenever the occasion calls for the dumps. Certainly there are fine qualities which war, despite its unnaturalness, develops. I'm hats off to every infantry private I meet nowadays.

God bless you and all of you.

Yours lovingly,
Con.

The reference in the previous letter to a cross is to a little bronze cross of Francis of Assisi.

Many years ago I visited Assisi, and, on leaving, the monks gave me four of these small bronze crosses, assuring me that those who wore them were securely defended in all peril by the efficacious prayers of St. Francis. Just before Coningsby left Shorncliff to go to France he wrote to us and asked if we couldn't send him something to hang round his neck for luck. We fortunately had one of these crosses of St. Francis at the ranch, and his sister--the M. of these letters-sent it to him. It arrived safely, and he has worn it ever since.

XI

September 15th, 1916.
DEAR FATHER:
Your last letter to me was written on a quiet morning in August--in the summer house at Kootenay. It came up yesterday evening on a water-cart from the wagon-lines to a scene a little in contrast.

It's a fortnight to-day since I left England, and already I've seen action. Things move quickly in this game, and it is a game--one which brings out both the best and the worst qualities in a man. If unconscious heroism is the virtue most to be desired, and heroism spiced with a strong sense of humour at that, then pretty well every man I have met out here has the amazing guts to wear his crown of thorns as though it were a cap-and-bells. To do that for the sake of corporate stout-heartedness is, I think, the acme of what Aristotle meant by virtue. A strong man, or a good man or a brainless man, can walk to meet pain with a smile on his mouth because he knows that he is strong enough to bear it, or worthy enough to defy it, or because he is such a fool that he has no imagination. But these chaps are neither particularly strong, good, nor brainless; they're more like children, utterly casual with regard to trouble, and quite aware that it is useless to struggle against their elders. So they have the merriest of times while they can, and when the governess, Death, summons them to bed, they obey her with unsurprised quietness. It sends the mercury of one's optimism rising to see the way they do it. I search my mind to find the bigness of motive which supports them, but it forever evades me. These lads are not the kind who philosophise about life; they're the sort, many of them, who would ordinarily wear corduroys and smoke a cutty pipe. I suppose the Christian martyrs would have done the same had corduroys been the fashion in that day, and if a Roman Raleigh had discovered tobacco.

I wrote this about midnight and didn't get any further, as I was up till six carrying on and firing the battery. After adding another page or two I want to get some sleep, as I shall probably have to go up to the observation station to watch the effect of fire to-night. But before I turn in I want to tell you that I had the most gorgeous mail from everybody. Now that I'm in touch with you all again, it's almost like saying "How-do?" every night and morning.

I daresay you'll wonder how it feels to be under shell-fire. This is how it feels--you don't realise your danger until you come to think about it afterwards--at the time it's like playing coconut shies at a coon's head--only you're the coon's head. You take too much interest in the sport of dodging to be afraid. You'll hear the Tommies saying if one bursts nearly on them, "Line, you blighter, line. Five minutes more left," just as though they were reprimanding the unseen Hun battery for rotten shooting.

The great word of the Tommies here is "No bloody bon"--a strange mixture of French and English, which means that a thing is no good. If it pleases them it's *Jake*--though where Jake comes from nobody knows.

Now I must get a wink or two, as I don't know when I may have to start off.

Ever yours, with love,
CON.

XII

September 19th, 1916.

Dearest Mother:

I've been in France 19 days, and it hasn't taken me long to go into action. Soon I shall be quite an old hand. I'm just back from 24 hours in the Observation Post, from which one watches the effect of fire. I understand now and forgive the one phrase which the French children have picked up from our Tommies on account of its frequent occurrence--"bl---- mud." I never knew that mud could be so thick and treacly. All my fear that I might be afraid under shell-fire is over--you get to believe that if you're going to be hit you're going to be. But David's phrase keeps repeating itself in my mind, "Ten thousand shall fall at thy side, etc., but it shall not come nigh unto thee." It's a curious thing that the men who are most afraid are those who get most easily struck. A friend of G.M.C.'s was hit the other day within thirty yards of me--he was a Princeton chap. I mentioned him in one of my previous letters. Our right section commander got a blighty two days ago and is probably now in England. He went off on a firing battery wagon, grinning all over his face, saying he wouldn't sell that bit of blood and shrapnel for a thousand pounds. I'm wearing your tie--it's the envy of the battery. All the officers wanted me to give them the name of my girl. It never occurs to men that mothers will do things like that.

Thank the powers it has stopped raining and we'll be able to get dry. I came in plastered from head to foot with lying in the rain on my tummy and peering over the top of a trench. Isn't it a funny change from comfortable breakfasts, press notices and a blazing fire?

Do you want any German souvenirs? Just at present I can get plenty. I have a splendid bayonet and a belt with Kaiser Bill's arms on it--but you can't forward these things from France. The Germans swear that they're not using bayonets with saw-edges, but you can buy them for five francs from the Tommies--ones they've taken from the prisoners or else picked up.

You needn't be nervous about me. I'm a great little dodger of whizz-bangs. Besides I have a superstition that there's something in the power of M.'s cross to bless.

It came with the mittens, and is at present round my neck.

You know what it sounds like when they're shooting coals down an iron run-way into a cellar-well, imagine a thousand of them. That's what I'm hearing while I write.

God bless you; I'm very happy.

Yours ever,
Con.

XIII

September 19th, 1916.
Dearest Father:

I'm writing you your birthday letter early, as I don't know how busy I may be in the next week, nor how long this may take to reach you. You know how much love I send you and how I would like to be with you. D'you remember the birthday three years ago when we set the victrola going outside your room door? Those were my high-jinks days when very many things seemed possible. I'd rather be the person I am now than the person I was then. Life was selfish though glorious.

Well, I've seen my first modern battlefield and am quite disillusioned about the splendour of war. The splendour is all in the souls of the men who creep through the squalor like vermin--it's in nothing external. There was a chap here the other day who deserved the V.C. four times over by running back through the Hun shell fire to bring news that the infantry wanted more artillery support. I was observing for my brigade in the forward station at the time. How he managed to live through the ordeal nobody knows. But men laugh while they do these things. It's fine.

A modern battlefield is the abomination of abominations. Imagine a vast stretch of dead country, pitted with shell-holes as though it had been mutilated with small-pox. There's not a leaf or a blade of grass in sight. Every house has either been leveled or is in ruins. No bird sings. Nothing stirs. The only live sound is at night--the scurry of rats. You enter a kind of ditch, called a trench; it leads on to another and another in an unjoyful maze. From the sides feet stick out, and arms and faces--the dead of previous encounters. "One of our chaps," you say casually, recognising him by his boots or khaki, or "Poor blighter--a Hun!" One can afford to forget enmity in the presence of the dead. It is horribly difficult sometimes to distinguish between the living and the slaughtered--they both lie so silently in their little kennels in the earthen bank. You push on--especially if you are doing observation work, till you are past your own front line and out in No Man's Land. You have to crouch and move warily now. Zing! A bullet from a German sniper. You laugh and whisper, "A near one, that." My first trip to the trenches was up to No Man's Land. I went in the early dawn and came to a Madame Tussaud's show of the dead, frozen into immobility in the most extraordinary attitudes. Some of them were part way out of the ground, one hand pressed to the wound, the other pointing, the head sunken and the hair plastered over the forehead by repeated rains. I kept on wondering what my companions would look like had they been three weeks dead. My imagination became ingeniously and vividly morbid. When I had to step over them to pass, it seemed as though they must clutch at my trench coat and ask me to help. Poor lonely people, so brave and so anonymous in their death! Somewhere there is a woman who loved each one of them and would give her life for my opportunity to touch the poor clay that had been kind to her. It's like walking through the day of resurrection to visit No Man's Land. Then the Huns see you and the shrapnel begins to fall--you crouch like a dog and run for it.

One gets used to shell-fire up to a point, but there's not a man who doesn't want to duck when he hears one coming. The worst of all is the whizz-bang, because it doesn't give you a chance--it pounces and is on you the same moment that it bangs. There's so much I wish that I could tell you. I can only say this, at the moment we're making history.

What a curious birthday letter! I think of all your other birthdays--the ones before I met these silent men with the green and yellow faces, and the blackened lips which will never speak again. What happy times we have had as a family--what happy jaunts when you took me in those early days, dressed in a sailor suit, when you went hunting pictures. Yet, for all the damnability of what I now witness, I was never quieter in my heart. To have surrendered to an imperative self-denial brings a peace which self-seeking never brought.

So don't let this birthday be less gay for my absence. It ought to be the proud-est in your life--proud because your example has taught each of your sons to do the difficult things which seem right. It would have been a condemnation of you if any one of us had been a shirker.

"I want to buy fine things for you
And be a soldier if I can."

The lines come back to me now. You read them to me first in the dark little study from a green oblong book. You little thought that I would be a soldier--even now I can hardly realise the fact. It seems a dream from which I shall wake up. Am I really killing men day by day? Am I really in jeopardy myself?
Whatever happens I'm not afraid, and I'll give you reason to be glad of me.

Very much love,
CON.

The poem referred to in this letter was actually written for Coningsby when he was between five and six years old. The dark little study which he describes was in the old house at Wesley's Chapel, in the City Road, London--and it was very dark, with only one window, looking out upon a dingy yard. The green oblong book in which I used to write my poems I still have; and it is an illustration of the tenac-ity of a child's memory that he should recall it. The poem was called *A Little Boy's Programme*, and ran thus:

I am so very young and small,
That, when big people pass me by,
I sometimes think they are so high
I'll never be a man at all.

And yet I want to be a man
Because so much I want to do;
I want to buy fine things for you,

And be a soldier, if I can.

When I'm a man I will not let
Poor little children starve, or be
Ill-used, or stand and beg of me
With naked feet out in the wet.

Now, don't you laugh!--The father kissed
The little serious mouth and said
"You've almost made me cry instead,
You blessed little optimist."

XIV

September 21st, 1916.

My Very Dear M.:

I am wearing your talisman while I write and have a strong superstition in its efficacy. The efficacy of your socks is also very noticeable--I wore them the first time on a trip to the Forward Observation Station. I had to lie on my tummy in the mud, my nose just showing above the parapet, for the best part of twenty-four hours. Your socks little thought I would take them into such horrid places when you made them.

Last night both the King and Sir Sam sent us congratulations--I popped in just at the right time. I daresay you know far more about our doings than I do. Only this morning I picked up the *London Times* and read a full account of everything I have witnessed. The account is likely to be still fuller in the New York papers.

"Home for Christmas"--that's what the Tommies are promising their mothers and sweethearts in all their letters that I censor. Yesterday I was offered an Imperial commission in the army of occupation. But home for Christmas, will be Christmas, 1917--I can't think that it will be earlier.

Very much love, CON.

XV

Sunday, September 24th, 1916.

DEAREST MOTHER:

Your locket has just reached me, and I have strung it round my neck with M.'s cross. Was it M.'s cross the other night that accounted for my luck? I was in a gun-pit when a shell landed, killing a man only a foot away from me and wounding three others--I and the sergeant were the only two to get out all right. Men who have been out here some time have a dozen stories of similar near squeaks. And talking of squeaks, it was a mouse that saved one man. It kept him awake to such an extent that he determined to move to another place. Just as he got outside the dug-out a shell fell on the roof.

You'll be pleased to know that we have a ripping chaplain or Padre, as they call chaplains, with us. He plays the game, and I've struck up a great friendship with him. We discuss literature and religion when we're feeling a bit fed up. We talk at home of our faith being tested--one begins to ask strange questions here when he sees what men are allowed by the Almighty to do to one another, and so it's a fine thing to be in constant touch with a great-hearted chap who can risk his life daily to speak of the life hereafter to dying Tommies.

I wish I could tell you of my doings, but it's strictly against orders. You may read in the papers of actions in which I've taken part and never know that I was there.

We live for the most part on tinned stuff, but our appetites make anything taste palatable. Living and sleeping in the open air keeps one ravenous. And one learns to sleep the sleep of the just despite the roaring of the guns.

God bless you each one and give us peaceful hearts.

Yours ever,
Con.

XVI

September 28th, 1916.

My Dears:

We're in the midst of a fine old show, so I don't get much opportunity for writing. Suffice it to say that I've seen the big side of war by now and the extraordinary uncalculating courage of it. Men run out of a trench to an attack with as much eagerness as they would display in overtaking a late bus. If you want to get an idea of what meals are like when a row is on, order the McAlpin to spread you a table where 34th crosses Broadway--and wait for the uptown traffic on the Elevated. It's wonderful to see the waiters dodging with dishes through the shell-holes.

It's a wonderful autumn day, golden and mellow; I picture to myself what this country must have looked like before the desolation of war struck it.

I was Brigade observation officer on September 26th, and wouldn't have missed what I saw for a thousand dollars. It was a touch and go business, with shells falling everywhere and machine-gun fire--but something glorious to remember. I had the great joy of being useful in setting a Hun position on fire. I think the war will be over in a twelvemonth.

Our great joy is composing menus of the meals we'll eat when we get home. Good-bye for the present.

CON.

XVII

October 1st, 1916.

MY DEAREST M.:

Sunday morning, your first back in Newark. You're not up yet owing to the difference in time--I can imagine the quiet house with the first of the morning stealing greyly in. You'll be presently going to church to sit in your old-fashioned mahogany pew. There's not much of Sunday in our atmosphere--only the little one can manage to keep in his heart. I shall share the echo of yours by remembering.

I'm waiting orders at the present moment to go forward with the Colonel and pick out a new gun position. You know I'm very happy-satisfied for the first time I'm doing something big enough to make me forget all failures and self-contempts. I know at last that I can measure up to the standard I have always coveted for my-self. So don't worry yourselves about any note of hardship that you may interpret into my letters, for the deprivation is fully compensated for by the winged sense of exaltation one has.

Things have been a little warm round us lately. A gun to our right, another to our rear and another to our front were knocked out with direct hits. We've got some of the chaps taking their meals with us now because their mess was all shot to blazes. There was an officer who was with me at the 53rd blown thirty feet into the air while I was watching. He picked himself up and insisted on carrying on, al-though his face was a mass of bruises. I walked in on the biggest engagement of the entire war the moment I came out here. There was no gradual breaking-in for me. My first trip to the front line was into a trench full of dead.

Have you seen Lloyd George's great speech? I'm all with him. No matter what the cost and how many of us have to give our lives, this War must be so finished that war may be forever at an end. If the devils who plan wars could only see the abys-mal result of their handiwork! Give them one day in the trenches under shell-fire when their lives aren't worth a five minutes' purchase--or one day carrying back the wounded through this tortured country, or one day in a Red Cross train. No one can imagine the damnable waste and Christlessness of this battering of human flesh.

The only way that this War can be made holy is by making it so thorough that war will be finished for all time.

Papa at least will be awake by now. How familiar the old house seems to me--I can think of the place of every picture. Do you set the victrola going now-a-days? I bet you play Boys in Khaki, Boys in Blue.

Please send me anything in the way of eatables that the goodness of your hearts can imagine--also smokes.

Later.

I came back from the front-line all right and have since been hard at it firing. Your letters reached me in the midst of a bombardment--I read them in a kind of London fog of gun-powder smoke, with my steel helmet tilted back, in the interval of commanding my section through a megaphone.

Don't suppose that I'm in any way unhappy--I'm as cheerful as a cricket and do twice as much hopping--I have to. There's something extraordinarily bracing about taking risks and getting away with it--especially when you know that you're contributing your share to a far-reaching result. My mother is the mother of a soldier now, and soldiers' mothers don't lie awake at night imagining--they just say a prayer for their sons and leave everything in God's hands. I'm sure you'd far rather I died than not play the man to the fullest of my strength. It isn't when you die that matters--it's how. Not but what I intend to return to Newark and make the house reek of tobacco smoke before I've done.

We're continually in action now, and the casualty to B. has left us short-handed--moreover we're helping out another battery which has lost two officers. As you've seen by the papers, we've at last got the Hun on the run. Three hundred passed me the other day unescorted, coming in to give themselves up as prisoners. They're the dirtiest lot you ever set eyes on, and looked as though they hadn't eaten for months. I wish I could send you some souvenirs. But we can't send them out of France.

I'm scribbling by candlelight and everything's jumping with the stamping of the guns. I wear the locket and cross all the time.

Yours with much love,
Con.

XVIII

October 13th, 1916.

DEAR ONES:

I have only time to write and assure you that I am safe. We're living in trenches at present--I have my sleeping bag placed on a stretcher to keep it fairly dry. By the time you get this we expect to be having a rest, as we've been hard at it now for an unusually long time. How I wish that I could tell you so many things that are big and vivid in my mind-but the censor--!

Yesterday I had an exciting day. I was up forward when word came through that an officer still further forward was wounded and he'd been caught in a heavy enemy fire. I had only a kid telephonist with me, but we found a stretcher, went forward and got him out. The earth was hopping up and down like pop-corn in a frying pan. The unfortunate thing was that the poor chap died on the way out. It was only the evening before that we had dined together and he had told me what he was going to do with his next leave.

God bless you all,
CON.

XIX

October 14th, 1916.

DEAREST MOTHER:

I'm still all right and well. To-day I had the funniest experience of my life-- got caught in a Hun curtain of fire and had to lie on my tummy for two hours in a trench with the shells bursting five yards from me--and never a scratch. You know how I used to wonder what I'd do under such circumstances. Well, I laughed. All I could think of was the sleek people walking down Fifth Avenue, and the equally sleek crowds taking tea at the Waldorf. It struck me as ludicrous that I, who had been one of them, should be lying there lunchless. For a little while I was slightly deaf with the concussions.

That poem keeps on going through my head,

Oh, to come home once more, when the dusk is falling,
To see the nursery lighted and the children's table spread;
"Mother, mother, mother!" the eager voices calling,
"The baby was so sleepy that he had to go to bed!"
Wouldn't it be good, instead of sitting in a Hun dug-out?

Yours lovingly,
CON.

XX

October 15th, 1916.
Dear Ones:
We're still in action, but are in hopes that soon we may be moved to winter quarters. We've had our taste of mud, and are anxious to move into better quarters before we get our next. I think I told you that our O.C. had got wounded in the feet, and our right section commander got it in the shoulder a little earlier--so we're a bit short-handed and find ourselves with plenty of work.

I have curiously lucid moments when recent happenings focus themselves in what seems to be their true perspective. The other night I was Forward Observation officer on one of our recent battlefields. I had to watch the front all night for signals, etc. There was a full white moon sailing serenely overhead, and when I looked at it I could almost fancy myself back in the old melancholy pomp of autumn woodlands where the leaves were red, not with the colour of men's blood. My mind went back to so many by-gone days-especially to three years ago. I seemed so vastly young then, upon reflection. For a little while I was full of regrets for many things wasted, and then I looked at the battlefield with its scattered kits and broken rifles. Nothing seemed to matter very much. A rat came out-then other rats. I stood there feeling extraordinarily aloof from all things that can hurt, and--you'll smile--I planned a novel. O, if I get back, how differently I shall write! When you've faced the worst in so many forms, you lose your fear and arrive at peace. There's a marvellous grandeur about all this carnage and desolation--men's souls rise above the distress--they have to in order to survive. When you see how cheap men's bodies are you cannot help but know that the body is the least part of personality.

You can let up on your nervousness when you get this, for I shall almost certainly be in a safer zone. We've done more than our share and must be withdrawn soon. There's hardly a battery which does not deserve a dozen D.S.O.'s with a V.C. or two thrown in.

It's 4.30 now--you'll be in church and, I hope, wearing my flowers. Wait till I come back and you shall go to church with the biggest bunch of roses that ever were pinned to a feminine chest. I wonder when that will be.

We have heaps of humour out here. You should have seen me this morning, sitting on the gun-seat while my batman cut my hair. A sand-bag was spread over my shoulders in place of a towel and the gun-detachment stood round and gave advice. I don't know what I look like, for I haven't dared to gaze into my shaving mirror.

Good luck to us all,
CON

XXI

October 18th, 1910
Dearest M.:
I've come down to the lines to-day; to-morrow I go back again. I'm sitting alone in a deep chalk dug-out--it is 10 p.m. and I have lit a fire by splitting wood with a bayonet. Your letters from Montreal reached me yesterday. They came up

in the water-cart when we'd all begun to despair of mail. It was wonderful the silence that followed while every one went back home for a little while, and most of them met their best girls. We've fallen into the habit of singing in parts. Jerusalem the Golden is a great favourite as we wait for our breakfast--we go through all our favourite songs, including Poor Old Adam Was My Father. Our greatest favourite is one which is symbolising the hopes that are in so many hearts on this greatest battlefield in history. We sing it under shell-fire as a kind of prayer, we sing it as we struggle knee-deep in the appalling mud, we sing it as we sit by a candle in our deep captured German dug-outs. It runs like this:

> "There's a long, long trail a-winding
> Into the land of my dreams,
> Where the nightingales are singing
> And a white moon beams:
>
> There's a long, long night of waiting
> Until my dreams all come true;
> Till the day when I'll be going down
> That long, long trail with you."

You ought to be able to get it, and then you will be singing it when I'm doing it.

No, I don't know what to ask from you for Christmas--unless a plum pudding and a general surprise box of sweets and food stuffs. If you don't mind my suggesting it, I wouldn't a bit mind a Christmas box at once--a schoolboy's tuck box. I wear the locket, cross, and tie all the time as kind of charms against danger--they give me the feeling of loving hands going with me everywhere.

> God bless you.
> Yours ever,
> CON.

XXII

October 23, 1916

Dearest All:

As you know I have been in action ever since I left England and am still. I've lived in various extemporised dwellings and am at present writing from an eight foot deep hole dug in the ground and covered over with galvanised iron and sand-bags. We have made ourselves very comfortable, and a fire is burning--I correct that--comfortable until it rains, I should say, when the water finds its own level. We have just finished with two days of penetrating rain and mist--in the trenches the mud was up to my knees, so you can imagine the joy of wading down these shell-torn tunnels. Good thick socks have been priceless.

You'll be pleased to hear that two days ago I was made Right Section Com-mander--which is fairly rapid promotion. It means a good deal more work and responsibility, but it gives me a contact with the men which I like.

I don't know when I'll get leave--not for another two months anyway. It would be ripping if I had word in time for you to run over to England for the brief nine days.

I plan novels galore and wonder whether I shall ever write them the way I see them now. My imagination is to an extent crushed by the stupendousness of reality. I think I am changed in some stern spiritual way--stripped of flabbiness. I am per-haps harder--I can't say. That I should be a novelist seems unreasonable--it's so long since I had my own way in the world and met any one on artistic terms. But I have enough ego left to be very interested in my book. And by the way, when we're out at the front and the battery wants us to come in they simply phone up the password, "Slaves of Freedom," the meaning of which we all understand.

You are ever in my thoughts, and I pray the day may not be far distant when we meet again.

CON.

XXIII

October 27th, 1916.

Dearest Family:

All to-day I've been busy registering our guns. There is little chance of rest--one would suppose that we intended to end the war by spring.

Two new officers joined our battery from England, which makes the work lighter. One of them brings the news that D., one of the two officers who crossed over from England with me and wandered through France with me in search of our Division, is already dead. He was a corking fellow, and I'm very sorry. He was caught by a shell in the head and legs.

I am still living in a sand-bagged shell-hole eight feet beneath the level of the ground. I have a sleeping bag with an eider-down inside it, for my bed; it is laid on a stretcher, which is placed in a roofed-in trench. For meals, when there isn't a block on the roads, we do very well; we subscribe pretty heavily to the mess, and have an officer back at the wagon-lines to do our purchasing. When we move forward into a new position, however, we go pretty short, as roads have to be built for the throng of traffic. Most of what we eat is tinned--and I never want to see tinned salmon again when this war is ended. I have a personal servant, a groom and two horses--but haven't been on a horse for seven weeks on account of being in action. We're all pretty fed up with continuous firing and living so many hours in the trenches. The way artillery is run to-day an artillery lieutenant is more in the trenches than an infantryman--the only thing he doesn't do is to go over the parapet in an attack. And one of our chaps did that the other day, charging the Huns with a bar of chocolate in one hand and a revolver in the other. I believe he set a fashion which will be imitated. Three times in my experience I have seen the infantry jump out of their trenches and go across. It's a sight never to be forgotten. One time there were machine guns behind me and they sent a message to me, asking me to lie down and take cover. That was impossible, as I was observing for my brigade, so I lay on the parapet till the bullets began to fall too close for comfort, then I dodged out into a shell-hole with the German barrage bursting all around me, and had a most gorgeous view of a modern attack. That was some time ago, so you needn't be nervous.

Have I mentioned rum to you? I never tasted it to my knowledge until I came out here. We get it served us whenever we're wet. It's the one thing which keeps a man alive in the winter--you can sleep when you're drenched through and never get a cold if you take it.

At night, by a fire, eight feet underground, we sing all the dear old songs. We manage a kind of glee--Clementina, The Long, Long Trail, Three Blind Mice, Long, Long Ago, Rock of Ages. Hymns are quite favourites.

Don't worry about me; your prayers weave round me a mantle of defence.

Yours with more love than I can write,

CON.

XXIV

October 31st, 1916. Hallowe'en.

Dearest People:

Once more I'm taking the night-firing and so have a chance to write to you. I got letters from you all, and they each deserve answers, but I have so little time to write. We've been having beastly weather--drowned out of our little houses below ground, with rivers running through our beds. The mud is once more up to our knees and gets into whatever we eat. The wonder is that we keep healthy--I suppose it's the open air. My throat never troubles me and I'm free from colds in spite of wet feet. The main disadvantage is that we rarely get a chance to wash or change our clothes. Your ideas of an army with its buttons all shining is quite erroneous; we look like drunk and disorderlies who have spent the night in the gutter--and we have the same instinct for fighting.

In the trenches the other day I heard mother's Suffolk tongue and had a jolly talk with a chap who shared many of my memories. It was his first trip in and the Huns were shelling badly, but he didn't seem at all upset.

We're still hard at it and have given up all idea of a rest--the only way we'll get one is with a blighty. You say how often you tell yourselves that the same moon looks down on me; it does, but on a scene how different! We advance over old battlefields--everything is blasted. If you start digging, you turn up what's left of something human. If there were any grounds for superstition, surely the places in which I have been should be ghost-haunted. One never thinks about it. For myself I have increasingly the feeling that I am protected by your prayers; I tell myself so when I am in danger.

Here I sit in an old sweater and muddy breeches, the very reverse of your picture of a soldier, and I imagine to myself your receipt of this. Our chief interest is to enquire whether milk, jam and mail have come up from the wagon-lines; it seems a faery-tale that there are places where milk and jam can be had for the buying. See how simple we become.

Poor little house at Kootenay! I hate to think of it empty. We had such good times there twelve months ago. They have a song here to a nursery rhyme lilt, Apres le Guerre Finis; it goes on to tell of all the good times we'll have when the war is ended. Every night I invent a new story of my own celebration of the event, usually, as when I was a kiddie, just before I fall asleep--only it doesn't seem possible that the war will ever end.

I hear from the boys very regularly. There's just the chance that I may get leave to London in the New Year and meet them before they set out. I always picture you with your heads high in the air. I'm glad to think of you as proud because of the pain we've made you suffer.

Once again I shall think of you on Papa's birthday. I don't think this will be the saddest he will have to remember. It might have been if we three boys had still all been with him. If I were a father, I would prefer at all costs that my sons should be men. What good comrades we've always been, and what long years of happy times we have in memory--all the way down from a little boy in a sailor-suit to Kootenay!

I fell asleep in the midst of this. I've now got to go out and start the other gun firing. With very much love.

Yours,

CON.

XXV

November 1st, 1916.

My Dearest M.:

Peace after a storm! Your letter was not brought up by the water-wagon this evening, but by an orderly--the mud prevented wheel-traffic. I was just sitting down to read it when Fritz began to pay us too much attention. I put down your letter, grabbed my steel helmet, rushed out to see where the shells were falling, and then cleared my men to a safer area. (By the way, did I tell you that I had been made Right Section Commander?) After about half an hour I came back and settled down by a fire made of smashed ammunition boxes in a stove borrowed from a ruined cottage. I'm always ashamed that my letters contain so little news and are so uninteresting. This thing is so big and dreadful that it does not bear putting down on paper. I read the papers with the accounts of singing soldiers and other rubbish; they depict us as though we were a lot of hair-brained idiots instead of men fully realising our danger, who plod on because it's our duty. I've seen a good many men killed by now--we all have--consequently the singing soldier story makes us smile. We've got a big job; we know that we've got to "Carry On" whatever happens--so we wear a stern grin and go to it. There's far more heroism in the attitude of men out here than in the footlight attitude that journalists paint for the public. It isn't a singing matter to go on firing a gun when gun-pits are going up in smoke within sight of you.

What a terrible desecration war is! You go out one week and look through your glasses at a green, smiling country-little churches, villages nestling among woods, white roads running across a green carpet; next week you see nothing but ruins and a country-side pitted with shell-holes. All night the machine guns tap like rivetting machines when a New York sky-scraper is in the building. Then suddenly in the night a bombing attack will start, and the sky grows white with signal rockets. Orders come in for artillery retaliation, and your guns begin to stamp the ground like stallions; in the darkness on every side you can see them snorting fire. Then stillness again, while Death counts his harvest; the white rockets grow fainter and less hysterical. For an hour there is blackness.

My batman consoles himself with singing,

"Pack up your troubles in your old kit-bag,
And smile, smile, smile."

There's a lot in his philosophy--it's best to go on smiling even when some one who was once your pal lies forever silent in his blanket on a stretcher.

The great uplifting thought is that we have proved ourselves men. In our death we set a standard which in ordinary life we could never have followed. Inevitably we should have sunk below our highest self. Here we know that the world will remember us and that our loved ones, in spite of tears, will be proud of us. What God will say to us we cannot guess--but He can't be too hard on men who did their duty. I think we all feel that trivial former failures are washed out by this final sacrifice. When little M. used to recite "Breathes there a man with soul so dead, who never to himself had said, 'This is my own, my native land,'" I never thought that I should have the chance that has now been given to me. I feel a great and solemn gratitude that I have been thought worthy. Life has suddenly become effective and worthy by reason of its carelessness of death.

By the way, that Princeton man I mentioned so long ago was killed forty yards away from me on my first trip into the trenches. Probably G. M'C. and his other friends know by now. He was the first man I ever saw snuffed out.

I'm wearing your mittens and find them a great comfort. I'll look forward to some more of your socks--I can do with plenty of them. If any of your friends are making things for soldiers, I wish you'd get them to send them to this battery, as they would be gratefully accepted by the men.

I wish I could come to *The Music Master* with you. I wonder how long till we do all those intimately family things together again.

Good-bye, my dearest M. I live for home letters and am rarely disappointed.

God bless you, and love to you all.

Yours ever,

CON.

XXVI

November 4th, 1916.

My Dearest Mother:

This morning I was wakened up in the gunpit where I was sleeping by the arrival of the most wonderful parcel of mail. It was really a kind of Christmas morning for me. My servant had lit a fire in a punctured petrol can and the place looked very cheery. First of all entered an enormous affair, which turned out to be a stove which C. had sent. Then there was a sand-bag containing all your gifts. You may bet I made for that first, and as each knot was undone remembered the loving hands that had done it up. I am now going up to a twenty-four-hour shift of observing, and shall take up the malted milk and some blocks of chocolate for a hot drink. It somehow makes you seem very near to me to receive things packed with your hands. When I go forward I shall also take candles and a copy of **Anne Veronica** with me, so that if I get a chance I can forget time.

Always when I write to you odds and ends come to mind, smacking of local colour. After an attack some months ago I met a solitary private wandering across a shell-torn field, I watched him and thought something was wrong by the aimlessness of his progress. When I spoke to him, he looked at me mistily and said, "Dead men. Moonlit road." He kept on repeating the phrase, and it was all that one could get out of him. Probably the dead men and the moonlit road were the last sights he had seen before he went insane.

Another touching thing happened two days ago. A Major turned up who had travelled fifty miles by motor lorries and any conveyance he could pick up on the road. He had left his unit to come to have a glimpse of our front-line trench where his son was buried. The boy had died there some days ago in going over the parapet. I persuaded him that he ought not to go alone, and that in any case it wasn't a healthy spot. At last he consented to let me take him to a point from which he could see the ground over which his son had attacked and led his men. The sun was sinking behind us. He stood there very straightly, peering through my glasses--and then forgot all about me and began speaking to his son in childish love-words.

"Gone West," they call dying out here--we rarely say that a man is dead. I found out afterwards that it was the boy's mother the Major was thinking of when he pledged himself to visit the grave in the front-line.

But there are happier things than that. For instance, you should hear us singing at night in our dug-out--every tune we ever learnt, I believe. Silver Threads Among the Gold, In the Gloaming, The Star of Bethlehem, I Hear You Calling Me, interspersed with Everybody Works but Father, and Poor Old Adam, etc.

I wish I could know in time when I get my leave for you to come over and meet me. I'm going to spend my nine days in the most glorious ways imaginable. To start with I won't eat anything that's canned and, to go on, I won't get out of bed till I feel inclined. And if you're there--!

Dreams and nonsense! God bless you all and keep us near and safe though absent. Alive or "Gone West" I shall never be far from you; you may depend on that--and I shall always hope to feel you brave and happy. This is a great game--cheese-mites pitting themselves against all the splendours of Death. Please, please write well ahead, so that I may not miss your Christmas letters.

Yours lovingly,
CON.

XXVII

November 6th, 1916.
My Dear Ones:
Such a wonderful day it has been--I scarcely know where to start. I came down last night from twenty-four hours in the mud, where I had been observing. I'd spent the night in a hole dug in the side of the trench and a dead Hun forming part of the roof. I'd sat there re-living so many things--the ecstatic moments of my life when I first touched fame--and my feet were so cold that I could not feel them, so I thought all the harder of the pleasant things of the past. Then, as I say, I came back to the gun position to learn that I was to have one day off at the back of the lines. You can't

imagine what that meant to me--one day in a country that is green, one day where there is no shell-fire, one day where you don't turn up corpses with your tread! For two months I have never left the guns except to go forward and I have never been from under shell-fire. All night long as I have slept the ground had been shaken by the stamping of the guns--and now after two months, to come back to comparative normality! The reason for this privilege being granted was that the powers that he had come to the conclusion that it was time I had a bath. Since I sleep in my clothes and water is too valuable for washing anything but the face and hands, they were probably right in their guess at my condition.

So with the greatest holiday of my life in prospect I went to the empty gun-pit in which I sleep, and turned in. This morning I set out early with my servant, tramping back across the long, long battlefields which our boys have won. The mud was knee-deep in places, but we floundered on till we came to our old and deserted gun-position where my horses waited for me. From there I rode to the wagon-lines--the first time I've sat a horse since I came into action. Far behind me the thunder of winged murder grew more faint. The country became greener; trees even had leaves upon them which fluttered against the grey-blue sky. It was wonderful--like awaking from an appalling nightmare. My little beast was fresh and seemed to share my joy, for she stepped out bravely.

When I arrived at the wagon-lines I would not wait--I longed to see something even greener and quieter. My groom packed up some oats and away we went again. My first objective was the military baths; I lay in hot water for half-an-hour and read the advertisements of my book. As I lay there, for the first time since I've been out, I began to get a half-way true perspective of myself. What's left of the egotism of the author came to life, and--now laugh--I planned my next novel--planned it to the sound of men singing, because they were clean for the first time in months. I left my towels and soap with a military policeman, by the roadside, and went prancing off along country roads in search of the almost forgotten places where people don't kill one another. Was it imagination? There seemed to me to be a different look in the faces of the men I met--for the time being they were neither hunters nor hunted. There were actually cows in the fields. At one point, where pollarded trees stand like a Hobbema sketch against the sky, a group of officers were coursing a hare, following a big black hound on horseback. We lost our way. A drenching rainstorm fell over us--we didn't care; and we saw as we looked back a most beautiful thing--a rainbow over green fields. It was as romantic as the first rainbow in childhood.

All day I have been seeing lovely and familiar things as though for the first time. I've been a sort of Lazarus, rising out of his tomb and praising God at the sound of a divine voice. You don't know how exquisite a ploughed field can look, especially after rain, unless you have feared that you might never see one again.

I came to a grey little village, where civilians were still living, and then to a gate and a garden. In the cottage was a French peasant woman who smiled, patted my hair because it was curly, and chattered interminably. The result was a huge omelette and a bottle of champagne. Then came a touch of naughtiness--a lady visitor with a copy of **La Vie Parisienne**, which she promptly bestowed on the English soldier. I read it, and dreamt of the time when I should walk the Champs Elysees again. It was growing dusk when I turned back to the noise of battle. There was a white moon in a milky sky. Motor-bikes fled by me, great lorries driven by Jehus from London buses, and automobiles which too poignantly had been Strand taxis and had taken lovers home from the Gaiety. I jogged along thinking very little, but supremely happy. Now I'm back at the wagon-line; to-morrow I go back to the guns. Meanwhile I write to you by a guttering candle.

Life, how I love you! What a wonderful kindly thing I could make of you to-night. Strangely the vision has come to me of all that you mean. Now I could write. So soon you may go from me or be changed into a form of existence which all my training has taught me to dread. After death is there only nothingness? I think that for those who have missed love in this life there must be compensations--the little children whom they ought to have had, perhaps. To-day, after so many weeks, I have seen little children again.

And yet, so strange a havoc does this war work that, if I have to "Go West," I shall go **proudly** and quietly. I have seen too many men die bravely to make a fuss if my turn comes. A mixed passenger list old Father Charon must have each night--Englishmen, Frenchmen, and Huns. To-morrow I shall have another sight of the greenness and then--the guns.

I don't know whether I have been able to make any of my emotions clear to you in my letters. Terror has a terrible fascination. Up to now I have always been afraid--afraid of small fears. At last I meet fear itself and it stings my pride into an unpremeditated courage.

I've just had a pile of letters from you all. How ripping it is to be remembered! Letters keep one civilised.

It's late and I'm very tired. God bless you each and all.

CON.

XXVIII

November 15th, 1916.

Dear Father:

I've owed you a letter for some time, but I've been getting very little leisure. You can't send steel messages to the Kaiser and love-notes to your family in the same breath.

I am amazed at the spirit you three are showing and almighty proud that you can muster such courage. I suppose none of us quite realised our strength till it came to the test. There was a time when we all doubted our own heroism. I think we were typical of our age. Every novel of the past ten years has been more or less a study in sentiment and self-distrust. We used to wonder what kind of stuff Drake's men were made of that they could jest while they died. We used to contrast ourselves with them to our own disfavour. Well, we know now that when there's a New World to be discovered we can still rise up reincarnated into spiritual pirates. It wasn't the men of our age who were at fault, but the New World that was lacking. Our New World is the Kingdom of Heroism, the doors of which are flung so wide that the meanest of us may enter. I know men out here who are the dependable daredevils of their brigades, who in peace times were nuisances and as soon as peace is declared will become nuisances again. At the moment they're fine, laughing at Death and smiling at the chance of agony. There's a man I know of who had a record sheet of crimes. When he was out of action he was always drunk and up for office. To get rid of him, they put him into the trench mortars and within a month he had won his D.C.M. He came out and went on the spree--this particular spree consisted in stripping a Highland officer of his kilts on a moonlight night. For this he was sentenced to several months in a military prison, but asked to be allowed to serve his sentence in the trenches. He came out from his punishment a King's sergeant--which means that whatever he did nobody could degrade him. He got this for lifting his trench mortar over the parapet when all the detachment were killed. Carrying it out into a shell-hole, he held back the Hun attack and saved the situation. He got drunk again, and again chose to be returned to the trenches. This time his head was blown off while he was engaged in a special feat of gallantry. What are you to say to such men? Ordinarily they'd be blackguards, but war lifts them into splendour. In the same way you see mild men, timid men, almost girlish men, carrying out duties which in other wars would have won V.C.'s. I don't think the soul of courage ever dies out of the race any more than the capacity for love. All it means is that the occasion is not present. For myself I try to analyse my emotions; am I simply numb, or do I imitate other people's coolness and shall I fear life again when the war is ended? There is no explanation save the great army phrase "Carry on." We "carry on" because, if we don't, we shall let other men down and put their lives in danger. And there's more than that--we all want to live up to the standard that prompted us to come.

One talks about splendour--but war isn't splendid except in the individual sense. A man by his own self-conquest can make it splendid for himself, but in the massed sense it's squalid. There's nothing splendid about a battlefield when the fight is ended--shreds of what once were men, tortured, levelled landscapes--the barbaric loneliness of Hell. I shall never forget my first dead man. He was a signalling officer, lying in the dawn on a muddy hill. I thought he was asleep at first, but when I looked more closely, I saw that his shoulder blade was showing white through his tunic. He was wearing black boots. It's odd, but the sight of black boots have the same effect on me now that black and white stripes had in childhood. I have the superstitious feeling that to wear them would bring me bad luck.

Tonight we've been singing in parts, Back in the Dear Dead Days Beyond Recall--a mournful kind of ditty to sing under the circumstances--so mournful that we had to have a game of five hundred to cheer us up.

It's now nearly 2 a.m., and I have to go out to the guns again before I go to bed. I carry your letters about in my pockets and read them at odd intervals in all kinds of places that you can't imagine.

Cheer up and remember that I'm quite happy. I wish you could be with me for just one day to understand.

Yours,
CON.

XXIX

December 3rd, 1916.

Dear Boys:

By this time you will be all through your exams and I hope have both passed. It'll be splendid if you can go together to the same station. You envy me, you say; well, I rather envy you. I'd like to be with you. You, at least, don't have Napoleon's fourth antagonist with which to contend--mud. But at present I'm clean and billeted in an estaminet, in a not too bad little village. There's an old mill and still older church, and the usual farmhouses with the indispensable pile of manure under the front windows. We shall have plenty of hard work here, licking our men into shape and re-fitting.

You know how I've longed to sleep between sheets; I can now, but find them so cold that I still use my sleeping bag--such is human inconsistency. But yesterday I had a boiling bath--as good a bath as could be found in a New York hotel--and I am CLEAN.

I woke up this morning to hear some one singing Casey Jones--consequently I thought of former Christmases. My mind has been travelling back very much of late. Suddenly I see something here which reminds me of the time when E. and I were at Lisieux, or even of our Saturday excursions to Nelson when we were all together at the ranch.

Did I tell you that B., our officer who was wounded two months ago, has just returned to us. This morning he got news that his young brother has been killed in the place which we have left. I wonder when we shall grow tired of stabbing and shooting and killing. It seems to me that the war cannot end in less than two years.

I have made myself nice to the Brigade interpreter and he has found me a delightful room with electric light and a fire. It's in an old farmhouse with a brick terrace in front. My room is on the ground floor and tile-paved. The chairs are rush-bottomed and there are old quaint china plates on the shelves. There is also a quite charming mademoiselle. So you see, you don't need to pity me any more.

Just at present I'm busy getting up the Brigade Christmas Entertainment. The Colonel asked me to do it, otherwise I should have said **no**, as I want all the time I can get to myself. You can't think how jolly it is to sit again in a room which is temporarily yours after living in dug-outs, herded side by side with other men. I can be **me** now, and not a soldier of thousands when I write. You shall hear from me again soon. Hope you're having a ripping time in London.

Yours ever,
CON.

XXX

December 5th, 1916.

DEAREST M.:

I've just come in from my last tour of inspection as orderly officer, and it's close on midnight. I'm getting this line off to you to let you know that I expect to get my nine days' leave about the beginning of January. How I wish it were possible to have you in London when I arrive, or, failing that, to spend my leave in New York!

To-morrow I make an early start on horseback for a market of the old-fashioned sort which is held at a town near by. Can you dimly picture me with my groom, followed by a mess-cart, going from stall to stall and bartering with the peasants? It'll be rather good fun and something quite out of my experience.

Christmas will be over by the time you get this, and I do hope that you had a good one. I paused to talk to the other officers; they say that they are sure that you are very beautiful and have a warm heart, and would like to send them a five-storey layer cake, half a dozen bottles of port and one Paris chef. At present I am the Dives of the mess and dole out luxuries to these Lazaruses.

Good-bye for the present.

Yours ever lovingly,
CON.

XXXI

December 6th, 1916.

Dearest M.:

I've just undone your Christmas parcels, and already I am wearing the waist-coat and socks, and my mouth is hot with the ginger.

I expect to get leave for England on January 10th. I do wish it might be possible for some of you to cross the ocean and be in London with me--and I don't see what there is to prevent you. Unless the war ends sooner than any of us expect, it is not likely that I shall get another leave in less than nine months. So, if you want to come and if there's time when you receive this letter, just hop on a boat and let's see what London looks like together.

I wonder what kind of a Christmas you'll have. I shall picture it all. You may hear me tiptoeing up the stairs if you listen very hard. Where does the soul go in sleep? Surely mine flies back to where all of you dear people are.

I came back to my farm yesterday to find a bouquet of paper flowers at the head of my bed with a note pinned on it. Over my fire-place was hung a pathetic pair of farm-girls' heavy Sunday boots, all brightly polished, with two other notes pinned on them. The Feast of St. Nicholas on December 7th is an opportunity for unmarried men to be reminded that there are unmarried girls in the world--wherefore the flowers. I enclose the notes. Keep them,--they may be useful for a book some day.

I'm having a pretty good rest, and am still in my old farmhouse.

Love to all.

CON.

XXXII

December 15th, 1916.

Dearest All:

At the present I'm just where mother hoped I'd be--in a deep dug-out about twenty feet down--we're trying to get a fire lighted, and consequently the place is smoked out. Where I'll be for Christmas I don't know, but I hope by then to be in billets. I've just come back from the trenches, where I've been observing. The mud is not nearly so bad where I am now, and with a few days' more work, we should be quite comfortable. You'll have received my cable about my getting leave soon--I'm wondering whether the Atlantic is sufficiently quiet for any of you to risk a crossing.

Poor Basil! Your letter was the first news I got of his death. I must have watched the attack in which he lost his life. One wonders now how it was that some instinct did not warn me that one of those khaki dots jumping out of the trenches was the cousin who stayed with us in London.

I'm wondering what this mystery of the German Chancellor is all about--some peace proposals, I suppose--which are sure to prove bombastic and unacceptable. It seems to us out here as though the war must go on forever. Like a boy's dream of the far-off freedom of manhood, the day appears when we shall step out into the old liberty of owning our own lives. What a celebration we'll have when I come home! I can't quite grasp the joy of it.

I've got to get this letter off quite soon if it's to go to-day. It ought to reach, you by January 12th or thereabouts. You may be sure my thoughts will have been with you on Christmas day. I shall look back and remember all the by-gone good times and then plan for Christmas, 1917. God keep us all.

Ever yours,
CON.

XXXIII

December 18th, 1916.

My Dearest M.:

I always feel when I write a joint letter to the family that I'm cheating each one of you, but it's so very difficult to get time to write as often as I'd like. It's a week to Christmas and I picture the beginnings of the preparations. I can look back and remember so many such preparations, especially when we were kiddies in London. What good times one has in a life! I've been sitting with my groom by the fire to-night while he dried my clothes. I've mentioned him to you before as having lived in Nelson, and worked at the Silver King mine. We both grew ecstatic over British Columbia. I am hoping all the time that the boys may be in England at the time I get my leave--I hardly dare hope that any of you will be there. But it would he grand if you could manage it--I long very much to see you all again. I can just imagine my first month home again. I shan't let any of you work. I shall be the incurable boy. I've spent the best part of to-day out in No Man's Land, within seventy yards of the Huns. Quite an experience, I assure you, and one that I wouldn't have missed for worlds. I'll have heaps to write into novels one day--the vividest kind of local colour. Just at present I have nothing to read but the Christmas number of the *Strand*. It makes me remember the time when we children raced for the latest development of *The Hound of the Baskervilles*, and so many occasions when I had one of "those sniffy colds" and sat by the Highbury fire with a book. Good days, those!

I'm just off to bed now, and will finish this to-morrow. Bed is my greatest luxury nowadays.

December 19th.

The book and chocolate just came, and a bunch of New York papers. All were most welcome. I was longing for something to read. To-morrow I have to go forward to observe. Two of our officers are on leave, so it makes the rest of us work pretty hard. What do you think of the Kaiser's absurd peace proposals? The man must be mad.

The best of love, CON.

XXXIV

December 20th, 1916.

Dear Mr. T.:

Just back from a successful argument with Fritz, to find your kind good wishes. It's rather a lark out here, though a lark which may turn against you any time. I laugh a good deal more than I mope. Anything really horrible has a ludicrous side-- it's like Mark Twain's humour--a gross exaggeration. The maddest thing of all to me is that a person so willing to be amiable as I am should be out here killing people for principle's sake. There's no rhyme or reason--it can't be argued. Dimly one thinks he sees what is right and leaves father and mother and home, as though it were for the Kingdom of Heaven's sake. Perhaps it is. If one didn't pin his faith to that "perhaps"--. One can't explain.

A merry Christmas to you.

Yours very sincerely,

CONINGSBY DAWSON.

XXXV

December 20th, 1916.

Dear Mr. A.D.:

I've just come in from an argument with Fritz when your chocolate formed my meal. You were very kind to think of me and to send it, and you were extraordinarily understanding in the letter that you sent me. One's life out here is like a pollarded tree--all the lower branches are gone--one gazes on great nobilities, on the fascinating horror of Eternity sometimes--I said horror, but it's often fine in its spaciousness--one gazes on many inverted splendours of Titans, but it's giddy work being so high and rarefied, and all the gentle past seems gone. That's why it is pleasant in this grimy anonymity of death and courage to get reminders, such as your letter, that one was once localised and had a familiar history. If I come back, I shall be like Rip Van Winkle, or a Robinson Crusoe--like any and all of the creatures of legend and history to whom abnormality has grown to seem normal. If you can imagine yourself living in a world in which every day is a demonstration of a Puritan's conception of what happens when the last trump sounds, then you have some idea of my queer situation. One has come to a point when death seems very inconsiderable and only failure to do one's duty is an utter loss. Love and the future, and all the sweet and tender dreams of by-gone days are like a house in which the blinds are lowered and from which the sight has gone. Landscapes have lost their beauty, everything God-made and man-made is destroyed except man's power to endure with a smile the things he once most dreaded, because he believes that only so may he be righteous in his own eyes. How one has longed for that sure confidence in the petty failings of little living--the confidence to believe that he can stand up and suffer for principle! God has given all men who are out here that opportunity--the supremest that can be hoped for--so, in spite of exile, Christmas for most of us will be a happy day. Does one see more truly life's worth on a battlefield? I often ask myself that question. Is the contempt that is hourly shown for life the real standard of life's worth? I shrug my shoulders at my own unanswerable questions--all I know is that I move daily with men who have everything to live for who, nevertheless, are urged by an unconscious magnanimity to die. I don't think any of our dead pity themselves--but they would have done so if they had faltered in their choice. One lives only from sunrise to sunrise, but there's a more real happiness in this brief living than I ever knew before, because it is so exactingly worth while.

Thank you again for your kindness.

Very sincerely yours,

C.D.

The suggestion that we might all meet in London in January, 1917, was a hope rather than an expectation. We received a cable from France on Sunday, December 17th, 1916, and left New York on December 30th. We were met in London by the two sailor-sons, who were expecting appointments at any moment, and Coningsby arrived late in the evening of January 13th. He was unwell when he arrived, having had a near touch of pneumonia. The day before he left the front he had been in action, with a temperature of 104. There were difficulties about getting his leave at the exact time appointed, but these he overcame by exchanging leave with a brother-officer. He travelled from the Front all night in a windowless train, and at Calais was delayed by a draft of infantry which he had to take over to England. The consequence of this delay was that the meeting at the railway station, of which he had so long dreamed, did not come off. We spent a long day, going from station to station, misled by imperfect information as to the arrival of troop trains. At Victoria Station we saw two thousand troops arrive on leave, men caked with trench-mud, but he was not among them. We reluctantly returned to our hotel in the late afternoon and gave up expecting him. There was all the time a telegram at the hotel from him, giving the exact place and time of his arrival, but it was not delivered until it was too late to meet him. He arrived at ten o'clock, and at the same time his two brothers, who had been summoned in the morning to Southampton, entered the hotel, having been granted special leave to return to London. A night's rest did wonders for Coningsby, and the next day his spirits were as high as in the old days of joyous holiday. During the next eight days we lived at a tense pitch of excitement. We went to theatres, dined in restaurants, met friends, and heard from his lips a hundred details of his life which could not be communicated in letters. We were all thrilled by the darkened heroic London through which we moved, the London which bore its sorrows so proudly, and went about its daily life with such silent courage. We visited old friends to whom the war had brought irreparable bereavements, but never once heard the voice of self-pity, of murmur or complaint. To me it was an incredible England; an England purged of all weakness, stripped of flabbiness, regenerated by sacrifice. I had dreamed of no such transformation by anything I had read in American newspapers and magazines. I think no one can imagine the completeness of this rebirth of the soul of England who has not dwelt, if only for a few days, among its people.

Coningsby's brief leave expired all too soon. We saw him off from Folkestone, and while we were saying good-bye to him, his two brothers were on their way to their distant appointments with the Royal Naval Motor Patrol in the North of Scotland. We left Liverpool for New York on January 27th, and while at sea heard of the diplomatic break between America and Germany. The news was received on board the *S.S. St. Paul* with rejoicing. It was Sunday, and the religious service on board concluded with the Star-Spangled Banner.

XXXVI

December 28th, 1916.

Dearest All:

I'm writing you this letter because I expect to-night is a busy-packing one with you. The picture is in my mind of you all. How splendid it is of you to come! I never thought you would really, not even in my wildest dream of optimism. There have been so many times when I scarcely thought that I would ever see you again--now the unexpected and hoped-for happens. It's ripping!

I've put in an application for special leave in case the ordinary leave should be cut off. I think I'm almost certain to arrive by the 11th. Won't we have a time? I wonder what we'll want to do most--sit quiet or go to theatres? The nine days of freedom--the wonderful nine days--will pass with most tragic quickness. But they'll be days to remember as long as life lasts.

Shall I see you standing on the station when I puff into London--or will it be Folkestone where we meet--or shall I arrive before you? I somehow think it will be you who will meet me at the barrier at Charing Cross, and we'll taxi through the darkened streets down the Strand, and back to our privacy. How impossible it sounds--like a vision of heart's desire in the night.

Far, far away I see the fine home-coming, like a lamp burning in a dark night. I expect we shall all go off our heads with joy and be madder than ever. Who in the old London days would have imagined such a nine days of happiness in the old places as we are to have together.

God bless you, till we meet,
CON.

XXXVII

January 4th, 1917.
10.30 p.m.
MY DEAREST ONES:

This letter is written to welcome you to England, but I may be with you when it is opened. It was glorious news to hear that you were coming--I was only playing a forlorn bluff when I sent those cables. You're on the sea at present and should be half way over. Our last trip over together you marvelled at the apparent indifference of the soldiers on board, and now you're coming to meet one of your own fresh from the Front. A change!

O what a nine days we're going to have together--the most wonderful that were ever spent. I dream of them, tell myself tales about them, live them over many times in imagination before they are realised. Sometimes I'm going to have no end of sleep, sometimes I'm going to keep awake every second, sometimes I'm going to sit quietly by a fire, and sometimes I'm going to taxi all the time. I can't fit your faces into the picture--it seems too unbelievable that we are to be together once again. To-day I've been staging our meeting--if you arrive first, and then if I arrive before you, and lastly if we both hit London on the same day. You mustn't expect me to be a sane person. You're three rippers to do this--and I hope you'll have an easy journey. The only ghost is the last day, when the leave train pulls out of Charing Cross. But we'll do that smiling, too; C'est la guerre.

Yours always and ever,
CON.

XXXVIII

January 6th, 1917.
MY DEAR ONES:

I have just seen a brother officer aboard the ex-London bus en route for Blighty. How I wished I could have stepped on board that ex-London perambulator to-night! "Pickerdilly Cirkuss, 'Ighbury, 'Ighgate, Welsh 'Arp--all the wye." O my, what a time I'll have when I meet you! I shall feel as though if anything happens to me after my return you'll be able to understand so much more bravely. These blinkered letters, with only writing and no touch of live hands, convey so little. When we've had a good time together and sat round the fire and talked interminably you'll be able to read so much more between the lines of my future letters. To-morrow you ought to land in England, and to-morrow night you should sleep in London. I am trying to swop my leave with another man, otherwise it won't come till the 15th. I am looking forward every hour to those miraculous nine days which we are to have together. You can't imagine with your vividest imagination the contrast between nine days with you in London and my days where I am now. A battalion went by yesterday, marching into action, and its band was playing I've a Sneakin' Feelin' in My Heart That I Want to Settle Down. We all have that sneaking feeling from time to time. I tell myself wonderful stories in the early dark mornings and become the architect of the most wonderful futures.

I'm coming to join you just as soon as I know how--at the worst I'll be in London on the 16th of this month.

Ever yours,
CON.

The following letters were written after Coningsby had met his family in London.

XXXIX

January 24th, 1917.

MY DEAR ONES:

I have had a chance to write you sooner than I expected, as I stopped the night where I disembarked, and am catching my train to-day.

It's strange to be back and under orders after nine days' freedom. Directly I landed I was detailed to march a party--it was that that made me lose my train--not that I objected, for I got one more sleep between sheets. I picked up on the boat in the casual way one does, with three other officers, so on landing we made a party to dine together, and had a very decent evening. I wasn't wanting to remember too much then, so that was why I didn't write letters.

What good times we have to look back on and how much to be thankful for, that we met altogether. Now we must look forward to the summer and, perhaps, the end of the war. What a mad joy will sweep across the world on the day that peace is declared!

This visit will have made you feel that you have a share in all that's happening over here and are as real a part of it as any of us. I'm awfully proud of you for your courage.

Yours lovingly,
CON.

XL

January 26th, 1917.

MY VERY DEAR ONES:

Here I am back--my nine days' leave a dream. I got into our wagon-lines last night after midnight, having had a cold ride along frozen roads through white wintry country. I was only half-expected, so my sleeping-bag hadn't been unpacked. I had to wake my batman and tramp about a mile to the billet; by the time I got there every one was asleep, so I spread out my sleeping-sack and crept in very quietly. For the few minutes before my eyes closed I pictured London, the taxis, the gay parties, the mystery of lights. I was roused this morning with the news that I had to go up to the gun-position at once. I stole just sufficient time to pick up a part of my accumulated mail, then got on my horse and set out. At the guns, I found that I was due to report as liaison officer, so here I am in the trenches again writing to you by candle-light. How wonderfully we have bridged the distance in spending those nine whole days together. And now it is over, and I am back in the trenches, and to-morrow you're sailing for New York.

I can't tell you what the respite has meant to me. There have been times when my whole past life has seemed a myth and the future an endless prospect of carrying on. Now I can distantly hope that the old days will return.

When I was in London half my mind was at the Front; now that I'm back in the trenches half my mind is in London. I re-live our gay times together; I go to cosy little dinners; I sit with you in the stalls, listening to the music; then I tumble off to sleep, and dream, and wake up to find the dream a delusion. It's a fine and manly contrast, however, between the game one plays out here and the fretful trivialities of civilian life.

XLI

January 27th.

I got as far as this and then "something" happened. Twenty-four hours have gone by and once more it's nearly midnight and I write to you by candle-light. Since last night I've been with these infantry boy-officers who are doing such great work in such a careless spirit of jolliness. Any softness which had crept into me during my nine days of happiness has gone. I'm glad to be out here and wouldn't wish to be anywhere else till the war is ended.

It's a week to-day since we were at *Charlie's Aunt*--such a cheerful little party!

I expect the boys are doing their share of remembering too somewhere on the sea at present. I know you are, as you round the coast of Ireland and set out for the Atlantic.

I've not been out of my clothes for three days and I've another day to go yet. I brought my haversack into the trenches with me; on opening it I found that some kind hands had slipped into it some clean socks and a bottle of Horlick's Malted Milk tablets.

The signallers in a near-by dug-out are singing Keep the Home-Fires Burning Till the Boys Come Home. That's what we're all doing, isn't it--you at your end and we at ours? The brief few days of possessing myself are over and once more stern duty lies ahead. But I thank God for the chance I've had to see again those whom I love, and to be able to tell them with my own lips some of the bigness of our life at the Front. No personal aims count beside the great privilege which is ours to carry on until the war is over.

All my thoughts are with you--so many memories of kindness. I keep on picturing things I ought to have done--things I ought to have told you. Always I can see, Oh, so vividly, the two sailor brothers waving good-bye as the train moved off through the London dusk, and then that other and forlorner group of three, standing outside the dock gates with the sentry like the angel in Eden, turning them back from happiness. With an extraordinary aloofness I watched myself moving like a puppet away from you whom I love most dearly in all the world--going away as if going were a thing so usual.

I'm asking myself again if there isn't some new fineness of spirit which will develop from this war and survive it. In London, at a distance from all this tragedy of courage, I felt that I had slipped back to a lower plane; a kind of flabbiness was creeping into my blood--the old selfish fear of life and love of comfort. It's odd that out here, where the fear of death should supplant the fear of life, one somehow rises into a contempt for everything which is not bravest. There's no doubt that the call for sacrifice, and perhaps the supreme sacrifice, can transform men into a nobility of which they themselves are unconscious. That's the most splendid thing of all, that they themselves are unaware of their fineness.

I'm now waiting to be relieved and am hurrying to finish this so that I may mail it as soon as I get back to the battery. There's a whole sack of letters and parcels waiting for me there, and I'm as eager to get to them as a kiddy to inspect his Christmas stocking. I always undo the string and wrappings with a kind of reverence, trying to picture the dear kneeling figures who did them up. In London I didn't dare to let myself go with you--I couldn't say all that was in my heart--it wouldn't have been wise. Don't ever doubt that the tenderness was there. Even though one is only a civilian in khaki, some of the soldier's sternness becomes second nature.

All the country is covered with snow--it's brilliant clear weather, more like America than Europe. I'm feeling strong as a horse, ever so much better than I felt when on leave. Life is really tremendously worth living, in spite of the war.

XLII

January 28th.

I'm back at the battery, sitting by a cosy fire. I might be up at Kootenay by the look of my surroundings. I'm in a shack with a really truly floor, and a window looking out on moonlit whiteness. If it wasn't for the tapping of the distant machine guns--tapping that always sounds to me like the nailing up of coffins--I might be here for pleasure. In imagination I can see your great ship, with all its portholes aglare, ploughing across the darkness to America. The dear sailor brothers I can't quite visualise; I can only see them looking so upright and pale when we said goodbye. It's getting late and the fire's dying. I'm half asleep; I've not been out of my clothes for three nights. I shall tell myself a story of the end of the war and our next meeting--it'll last from the time that I creep into my sack until I close my eyes. It's a glorious life.

Yours very lovingly,
CON

XLIII

January 31st, 1917.

DEAR MR. AND MRS. M.:

It was extremely good of you to remember me. I got back from leave in London on the 26th and found the cigarettes waiting for me. One hasn't got an awful lot of pleasures left, but smoking is one of them. I feel particularly doggy when I open my case and find my initials on them.

I expect you'll have heard all the news of my leave long before this reaches you. We had a splendid time and the greatest of luck. My sailor brothers were with me all but two days, and my people were in England only a few days before I arrived.

This is a queer adventure for a peaceable person like myself--it blots out all the past and reduces the future to a speck. One hardly hopes that things will ever be different, but looks forward to interminable years of carrying on. My leave rather corrected that frame of mind; it came as a surprise to be forced to realise that not all the world was living under orders on woman less, childless battlefields. But we don't need any pity--we manage our good times, and are sorry for the men who aren't here, for it's a wonderful thing to have been chosen to sacrifice and perhaps to die that the world of the future may be happier and kinder.

This letter is rather disjointed; I'm in charge of the battery for the time, and messages keep on coming in, and one has to rush out to give the order to fire.

It's an American night--snow-white and piercing, with a frigid moon sailing quietly. I think the quiet beauty of the sky is about the only thing in Nature that we do not scar and destroy with our fighting.

Good-bye, and thank you ever so much.

Yours very sincerely,
CONINGSBY DAWSON.

XLIV

February 1st, 1917.
11 p.m.
DEAR FATHER:

Your picture of the black days when no letter comes from me sets me off scribbling to you at this late hour. All to-day I've been having a cold but amusing time at the O.P. (Forward Observation Post). It seems brutal to say it, but taking potshots at the enemy when they present themselves is rather fun. When you watch them scattering like ants before the shell whose direction you have ordered, you somehow forget to think of them as individuals, any more than the bear-hunter thinks of the cubs that will be left motherless. You watch your victims through your glasses as God might watch his mad universe. Your skill in directing fire makes you what in peace times would be called a murderer. Curious! You're glad, and yet at close quarters only in hot blood would you hurt a man.

I'd been back for a little over an hour when I had to go forward again to guide in some guns. The country was dazzlingly white in the moonlight. As far as eye could see every yard was an old battlefield; beneath the soft white fleece of snow lay countless unburied bodies. Like frantic fingers tearing at the sky, all along the horizon, Hun lights were shooting up and drifting across our front. Tap-tap-tappity went the machine-guns; whoo-oo went the heavies, and they always stamp like angry bulls. I had to come back by myself across the heroic corruption which the snow had covered. All the way I asked myself why was I not frightened. What has happened to me? Ghosts should walk here if anywhere. Moreover, I know that I shall be frightened again when the war is ended. Do you remember how you once offered me money to walk through the Forest of Dean after dark, and I wouldn't? I wouldn't if you offered it to me now. You remember Meredith's lines in "The Woods of Westermain":

"All the eyeballs under hoods
Shroud you in their glare;

Enter these enchanted woods
You who dare."

Maybe what re-creates one for the moment is the British officer's uniform, and even more the fact that you are not asked, but expected, to do your duty. So I came back quite unruffled across battered trenches and silent mounds to write this letter to you.

My dear father, I'm over thirty, and yet just as much a little boy as ever. I still feel overwhelmingly dependent on your good opinion and love. I'm glad that they are black days when you have no letters from me. I love to think of the rush to the door when the postman rings and the excited shouting up the stairs, "Quick, one from Con."

February 2nd.

You see by the writing how tired I was when I reached this point. It's nearly twenty-four hours later and again night. The gramophone is playing an air from *La Tosca* to which the guns beat out a bass accompaniment. I close my eyes and picture the many times I have heard the (probably) German orchestras of Broadway Joy Palaces play that same music. How incongruous that I should be listening to it here and under these circumstances! It must have been listened to so often by gay crowds in the beauty places of the world. A romantic picture grows up in my mind of a blue night, the laughter of youth in evening dress, lamps twinkling through trees, far off the velvety shadow of water and mountains, and as a voice to it all, that air from *La Tosca*. I can believe that the silent people near by raise themselves up in their snow-beds to listen, each one recalling some ecstatic moment before the dream of life was shattered.

There's a picture in the Pantheon at Paris, I remember; I believe it's called *To Glory*. One sees all the armies of the ages charging out of the middle distance with Death riding at their head. The only glory that I have discovered in this war is in men's hearts--it's not external. Were one to paint the spirit of this war he would depict a mud landscape, blasted trees, an iron sky; wading through the slush and shell-holes would come a file of bowed figures, more like outcasts from the Embankment than soldiers. They're loaded down like pack animals, their shoulders are rounded, they're wearied to death, but they go on and go on. There's no "To

Glory" about what we're doing out here; there's no flash of swords or splendour of uniforms. There are only very tired men determined to carry on. The war will be won by tired men who could never again pass an insurance test, a mob of broken counter-jumpers, ragged ex-plumbers and quite unheroic persons. We're civilians in khaki, but because of the ideals for which we fight we've managed to acquire soldiers' hearts. My flow of thought was interrupted by a burst of song in which I was compelled to join. We're all writing letters around one candle; suddenly the O.C. looked up and began, God Be With You Till We Meet Again. We sang it in parts. It was in Southport, when I was about nine years old, that I first heard that sung. You had gone for your first trip to America, leaving a very lonely family behind you. We children were scared to death that you'd be drowned. One evening, coming back from a walk on the sand-hills, we heard voices singing in a garden, God Be With You Till We Meet Again. The words and the soft dusk, and the vague figures in the English summer garden, seemed to typify the terror of all partings. We've said good-bye so often since, and God has been with us. I don't think any parting was more hard than our last at the prosaic dock-gates with the cold wind of duty blowing, and the sentry barring your entrance, and your path leading back to America while mine led on to France. But you three were regular soldiers--just as much soldiers as we chaps who were embarking. One talks of our armies in the field, but there are the other armies, millions strong, of mothers and fathers and sisters, who keep their eyes dry, treasure muddy letters beneath their pillows, offer up prayers and wait, wait, wait so eternally for God to open another door.

To-morrow I again go forward, which means rising early and taking a long plod through the snows; that's one reason for not writing any more, and another is that our one poor candle is literally on its last legs.

Your poem, written years ago when the poor were marching in London, is often in my mind:

"Yesterday and to-day
Have been heavy with labour and sorrow;
I should faint if I did not see
The day that is after to-morrow."
And there's that last verse which prophesied utterly the spirit in which we

men at the Front are fighting to-day:

"And for me, with spirit elate
The mire and the fog I press thorough,
For Heaven shines under the cloud
Of the day that is after to-morrow."

We civilians who have been taught so long to love our enemies and do good to them who hate us--much too long ever to make professional soldiers--are watching with our hearts in our eyes for that day which conies after to-morrow. Meanwhile we plod on determinedly, hoping for the hidden glory.

Yours very lovingly,
Con.

XLV

February 3rd, 1917.
Dear Misses W.:
You were very kind to remember me at Christmas. **Seventeen** was read with all kinds of gusto by all my brother officers. It's still being borrowed.

I've been back from leave a few days now and am settling back to business again. It was a trifle hard after over-eating and undersleeping myself for nine days, and riding everywhere with my feet up in taxis. I was the wildest little boy. Here it's snowy and bitter. We wear scarves round our ears to keep the frost away and dream of fires a mile high. All I ask, when the war is ended, is to be allowed to sit asleep in a big armchair and to be left there absolutely quiet. Sleep, which we crave so much at times, is only death done up in sample bottles. Perhaps some of these very weary men who strew our battlefields are glad to lie at last at endless leisure.

Good-bye, and thank you.
Yours very sincerely, Con.

XLVI

February 4th, 1917.

My Dearest Mother:

Somewhere in the distance I can hear a piano going and men's voices singing A Perfect Day. It's queer how music creates a world for you in which you are not, and makes you dreamy. I've been sitting by a fire and thinking of all the happy times when the total of desire seemed almost within one's grasp. It never is--one always, always misses it and has to rub the dust from the eyes, recover one's breath and set out on the search afresh. I suppose when you grow very old you learn the lesson of sitting quiet, and the heart stops beating and the total of desire comes to you. And yet I can remember so many happy days, when I was a child in the summer and later at Kootenay. One almost thought he had caught the secret of carrying heaven in his heart.

By the time this reaches you I'll be in the line again, but for the present I'm undergoing a special course of training. You can't hear the most distant sound of guns, and if it wasn't for the pressure of study, similar to that at *Kingston*, one would be very rested.

Sunday of all days is the one when I remember you most. You're just sitting down to mid-day dinner,--I've made the calculation for difference of time. You're probably saying how less than a month ago we were in London. That doesn't sound true even when I write it. I wonder how your old familiar surroundings strike you. It's terrible to come down from the mountain heights of a great elation like our ten days in London. I often think of that with regard to myself when the war is ended. There'll be a sense of dissatisfaction when the old lost comforts are regained. There'll be a sense of lowered manhood. The stupendous terrors of Armageddon demand less courage than the uneventful terror of the daily commonplace. There's something splendid and exhilarating in going forward among bursting shells--we, who have done all that, know that when the guns have ceased to roar our blood will grow more sluggish and we'll never be such men again. Instead of getting up in the morning and hearing your O.C. say, "You'll run a line into trench so-and-so to-day and shoot up such-and-such Hun wire," you'll hear necessity saying, "You'll work from breakfast to dinner and earn your daily bread. And you'll do it to-morrow and to-morrow and to-morrow world without end. Amen." They never put that forever and forever part into their commands out here, because the Amen for any one of us may be only a few hours away. But the big immediate thing is so much easier to do than the prosaic carrying on without anxiety--which is your game. I begin to understand what you have had to suffer now that R. and E. are really at war too. I get awfully anxious about them. I never knew before that either of them owned so much of my heart. I get furious when I remember that they might get hurt. I've heard of a Canadian who joined when he learnt that his best friend had been murdered by Hun bayonets. He came to get his own back and was the most reckless man in his battalion. I can understand his temper now. We're all of us in danger of slipping back into the worship of Thor.

I'll write as often as I can while here, but I don't get much time--so you'll understand. It's the long nights when one sits up to take the firing in action that give one the chance to be a decent correspondent.

My birthday comes round soon, doesn't it? Good heavens, how ancient I'm getting and without any "grow old along with me" consolation. Well, to grow old is all in the job of living.

Good-bye, and God bless you all.

Yours ever,
Con.

XLVII

February 4th, 1917.

Dear Mr. B.:

I have been intending to write to you for a very long time, but as most of one's writing is done when one ought to be asleep, and sleep next to eating is one of our few remaining pleasures, my intended letter has remained in my head up to now. On returning from a nine days' leave to London the other day, however, I found two letters from you awaiting me and was reproached into effort.

War's a queer game--not at all what one's civilian mind imagined; it's far more horrible and less exciting. The horrors which the civilian mind dreads most are mutilation and death. Out here we rarely think about them; the thing which wears on one most and calls out his gravest courage is the endless sequence of physical discomfort. Not to be able to wash, not to be able to sleep, to have to be wet and cold for long periods at a stretch, to find mud on your person, in your food, to have to stand in mud, see mud, sleep in mud and to continue to smile--that's what tests courage. Our chaps are splendid. They're not the hair-brained idiots that some war-correspondents depict from day to day. They're perfectly sane people who know to a fraction what they're up against, but who carry on with a grim good-nature and a determination to win with a smile. I never before appreciated as I do to-day the latent capacity for big-hearted endurance that is in the heart of every man. Here are apparently quite ordinary chaps--chaps who washed, liked theatres, loved kiddies and sweethearts, had a zest for life--they're bankrupt of all pleasures except the supreme pleasure of knowing that they're doing the ordinary and finest thing of which they are capable. There are millions to whom the mere consciousness of doing their duty has brought an heretofore unexperienced peace of mind. For myself I was never happier than I am at present; there's a novel zip added to life by the daily risks and the knowledge that at last you're doing something into which no trace of selfishness enters. One can only die once; the chief concern that matters is *how* and not *when* you die. I don't pity the weary men who have attained eternal leisure in the corruption of our shell-furrowed battles; they "went West" in their supreme moment. The men I pity are those who could not hear the call of duty and whose consciences will grow more flabby every day. With the brutal roar of the first Prussian gun the cry came to the civilised world, "Follow thou me," just as truly as it did in Palestine. Men went to their Calvary singing Tipperary, rubbish, rhymed doggerel, but their spirit was equal to that of any Christian martyr in a Roman amphitheatre. "Greater love hath no man than this, that he lay down his life for his friend." Our chaps are doing that consciously, willingly, almost without bitterness towards their enemies; for the rest it doesn't matter whether they sing hymns or ragtime. They've followed their ideal--freedom--and died for it. A former age expressed itself in Gregorian chants; ours, no less sincerely, disguises its feelings in ragtime.

Since September I have been less than a month out of action. The game doesn't pall as time goes on--it fascinates. We've got to win so that men may never again be tortured by the ingenious inquisition of modern warfare. The winning of the war becomes a personal affair to the chaps who are fighting. The world which sits behind the lines, buys extra specials of the daily papers and eats three square meals a day, will never know what this other world has endured for its safety, for no man of this other world will have the vocabulary in which to tell. But don't for a moment mistake me--we're grimly happy.

What a serial I'll write for you if I emerge from this turmoil! Thank God, my outlook is all altered. I don't want to live any longer--only to live well.

Good-bye and good luck.

Yours,
Coningsby Dawson.

XLVIII

February 5th, 1917.

My Dearest Mother:

Aren't the papers good reading now-a-days with nothing to record but success? It gives us hope that at last, anyway before the year is out, the war must end. As you know, I am at the artillery school back of the lines for a month, taking an extra course. I have been meeting a great many young officers from all over the world and have listened to them discussing their program for when peace is declared. Very few of them have any plans or prospects. Most of them had just started on some course of professional training to which they won't have the energy to go back after a two years' interruption. The question one asks is how will all these men be reabsorbed into civilian life. I'm afraid the result will be a vast host of men with promising pasts and highly uncertain futures. We shall be a holiday world without an income. I'm afraid the hero-worship attitude will soon change to impatience when the soldiers beat their swords into ploughshares and then confess that they have never been taught to plough. That's where I shall score--by beating my sword into a pen. But what to write about--! Everything will seem so little and inconsequential after seeing armies marching to mud and death, and people will soon get tired of hearing about that. It seems as though war does to the individual what it does to the landscapes it attacks--obliterates everything personal and characteristic. A valley, when a battle has done with it, is nothing but earth--exactly what it was when God said, "Let there be Light;" a man just something with a mind purged of the past and ready to observe afresh. I question whether a return to old environments will ever restore to us the whole of our old tastes and affections. War is, I think, utterly destructive. It doesn't even create courage--it only finds it in the soul of a man. And yet there is one quality which will survive the war and help us to face the temptations of peace--that same courage which most of us have unconsciously discovered out here.

Well, my dear, I have little news--at least, none that I can tell. I'm just about recovered from an attack of "flu." I want to get thoroughly rid of it before I go back to my battery. I hope you all keep well. God bless you all.

Yours ever,
Con.

XLIX

February 6th, 1917.

My Very Dear M.:

I read in to-day's paper that U.S.A. threatens to come over and help us. I wish she would. The very thought of the possibility fills me with joy. I've been light-headed all day. It would be so ripping to live among people, when the war is ended, of whom you need not be ashamed. Somewhere deep down in my heart I've felt a sadness ever since I've been out here, at America's lack of gallantry--it's so easy to find excuses for not climbing to Calvary; sacrifice was always too noble to be sensible. I would like to see the country of our adoption become splendidly irrational even at this eleventh hour in the game; it would redeem her in the world's eyes. She doesn't know what she's losing. From these carcase-strewn fields of khaki there's a cleansing wind blowing for the nations that have died. Though there was only one Englishman left to carry on the race when this war is victoriously ended, I would give more for the future of England than for the future of America with her ninety millions whose sluggish blood was not stirred by the call of duty. It's bigness of soul that makes nations great and not population. Money, comfort, limousines and ragtime are not the requisites of men when heroes are dying. I hate the thought of Fifth Avenue, with its pretty faces, its fashions, its smiling frivolity. America as a great nation will die, as all coward civilisations have died, unless she accepts the stigmata of sacrifice, which a divine opportunity again offers her.

If it were but possible to show those ninety millions one battlefield with its sprawling dead, its pity, its marvellous forgetfulness of self, I think then--no, they wouldn't be afraid. Fear isn't the emotion one feels--they would experience the shame of living when so many have shed their youth freely. This war is a prolonged moment of exultation for most of us--we are redeeming ourselves in our own eyes. To lay down one's life for one's friend once seemed impossible. All that is altered.

We lay down our lives that the future generations may be good and kind, and so we can contemplate oblivion with quiet eyes. Nothing that is noblest that the Greeks taught is unpractised by the simplest men out here to-day. They may die childless, but their example will father the imagination of all the coming ages. These men, in the noble indignation of a great ideal, face a worse hell than the most ingenious of fanatics ever planned or plotted. Men die scorched like moths in a furnace, blown to atoms, gassed, tortured. And again other men step forward to take their places well knowing what will be their fate. Bodies may die, but the spirit of England grows greater as each new soul speeds upon its way. The battened souls of America will die and be buried. I believe the decision of the next few days will prove to be the crisis in America's nationhood. If she refuses the pain which will save her, the cancer of self-despising will rob her of her life.

This feeling is strong with us. It's past midnight, but I could write of nothing else to-night.

God bless you.

Yours ever,
Con.

The Codes Of Hammurabi And Moses
W. W. Davies

The discovery of the Hammurabi Code is one of the greatest achievements of archaeology, and is of paramount interest, not only to the student of the Bible, but also to all those interested in ancient history...

QTY

Religion **ISBN:** *1-59462-338-4* **Pages:132**
MSRP $12.95

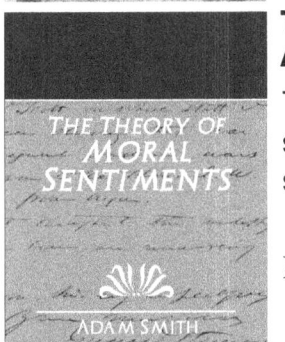

The Theory of Moral Sentiments
Adam Smith

This work from 1749. contains original theories of conscience amd moral judgment and it is the foundation for systemof morals.

QTY

Philosophy **ISBN:** *1-59462-777-0* **Pages:536**
MSRP $19.95

Jessica's First Prayer
Hesba Stretton

In a screened and secluded corner of one of the many railway-bridges which span the streets of London there could be seen a few years ago, from five o'clock every morning until half past eight, a tidily set-out coffee-stall, consisting of a trestle and board, upon which stood two large tin cans, with a small fire of charcoal burning under each so as to keep the coffee boiling during the early hours of the morning when the work-people were thronging into the city on their way to their daily toil...

QTY

Pages:84

Childrens **ISBN:** *1-59462-373-2* *MSRP $9.95*

My Life and Work
Henry Ford

QTY

Henry Ford revolutionized the world with his implementation of mass production for the Model T automobile. Gain valuable business insight into his life and work with his own auto-biography... "We have only started on our development of our country we have not as yet, with all our talk of wonderful progress, done more than scratch the surface. The progress has been wonderful enough but..."

Pages:300

Biographies/ **ISBN:** *1-59462-198-5* *MSRP $21.95*

The Art of Cross-Examination
Francis Wellman

QTY

I presume it is the experience of every author, after his first book is published upon an important subject, to be almost overwhelmed with a wealth of ideas and illustrations which could readily have been included in his book, and which to his own mind, at least, seem to make a second edition inevitable. Such certainly was the case with me; and when the first edition had reached its sixth impression in five months, I rejoiced to learn that it seemed to my publishers that the book had met with a sufficiently favorable reception to justify a second and considerably enlarged edition. ...

Reference   ISBN: *1-59462-647-2*

Pages:412

MSRP $19.95

On the Duty of Civil Disobedience
Henry David Thoreau

QTY

Thoreau wrote his famous essay, On the Duty of Civil Disobedience, as a protest against an unjust but popular war and the immoral but popular institution of slave-owning. He did more than write—he declined to pay his taxes, and was hauled off to gaol in consequence. Who can say how much this refusal of his hastened the end of the war and of slavery ?

Law   ISBN: *1-59462-747-9*

Pages:48

MSRP $7.45

Dream Psychology Psychoanalysis for Beginners
Sigmund Freud

QTY

Sigmund Freud, born Sigismund Schlomo Freud (May 6, 1856 - September 23, 1939), was a Jewish-Austrian neurologist and psychiatrist who co-founded the psychoanalytic school of psychology. Freud is best known for his theories of the unconscious mind, especially involving the mechanism of repression; his redefinition of sexual desire as mobile and directed towards a wide variety of objects; and his therapeutic techniques, especially his understanding of transference in the therapeutic relationship and the presumed value of dreams as sources of insight into unconscious desires.

Dream Psychology
Psychoanalysis for Beginners

Sigmund Freud

Psychology   ISBN: *1-59462-905-6*

Pages:196

MSRP $15.45

The Miracle of Right Thought
Orison Swett Marden

QTY

Believe with all of your heart that you will do what you were made to do. When the mind has once formed the habit of holding cheerful, happy, prosperous pictures, it will not be easy to form the opposite habit. It does not matter how improbable or how far away this realization may see, or how dark the prospects may be, if we visualize them as best we can, as vividly as possible, hold tenaciously to them and vigorously struggle to attain them, they will gradually become actualized, realized in the life. But a desire, a longing without endeavor, a yearning abandoned or held indifferently will vanish without realization.

Self Help   ISBN: *1-59462-644-8*

Pages:360

MSRP $25.45

QTY

The Rosicrucian Cosmo-Conception Mystic Christianity *by Max Heindel* ISBN: *1-59462-188-8* **$38.95**
The Rosicrucian Cosmo-conception is not dogmatic, neither does it appeal to any other authority than the reason of the student. It is: not controversial, but is: sent forth in the, hope that it may help to clear... New Age/Religion Pages 646

Abandonment To Divine Providence *by Jean-Pierre de Caussade* ISBN: *1-59462-228-0* **$25.95**
"The Rev. Jean Pierre de Caussade was one of the most remarkable spiritual writers of the Society of Jesus in France in the 18th Century. His death took place at Toulouse in 1751. His works have gone through many editions and have been republished... Inspirational Religion Pages 400

Mental Chemistry *by Charles Haanel* ISBN: *1-59462-192-6* **$23.95**
Mental Chemistry allows the change of material conditions by combining and appropriately utilizing the power of the mind. Much like applied chemistry creates something new and unique out of careful combinations of chemicals the mastery of mental chemistry... New Age Pages 354

The Letters of Robert Browning and Elizabeth Barret Barrett 1845-1846 vol II ISBN: *1-59462-193-4* **$35.95**
by Robert Browning and Elizabeth Barrett Biographies Pages 596

Gleanings In Genesis (volume I) *by Arthur W. Pink* ISBN: *1-59462-130-6* **$27.45**
Appropriately has Genesis been termed "the seed plot of the Bible" for in it we have, in germ form, almost all of the great doctrines which are afterwards fully developed in the books of Scripture which follow... Religion/Inspirational Pages 420

The Master Key *by L. W. de Laurence* ISBN: *1-59462-001-6* **$30.95**
In no branch of human knowledge has there been a more lively increase of the spirit of research during the past few years than in the study of Psychology, Concentration and Mental Discipline. The requests for authentic lessons in Thought Control, Mental Discipline and... New Age/Business Pages 422

The Lesser Key Of Solomon Goetia *by L. W. de Laurence* ISBN: *1-59462-092-X* **$9.95**
This translation of the first book of the "Lernegton" which is now for the first time made accessible to students of Talismanic Magic was done, after careful collation and edition, from numerous Ancient Manuscripts in Hebrew, Latin, and French... New Age/Occult Pages 92

Rubaiyat Of Omar Khayyam *by Edward Fitzgerald* ISBN:*1-59462-332-5* **$13.95**
Edward Fitzgerald, whom the world has already learned, in spite of his own efforts to remain within the shadow of anonymity, to look upon as one of the rarest poets of the century, was born at Bredfield, in Suffolk, on the 31st of March, 1809. He was the third son of John Purcell... Music Pages 172

Ancient Law *by Henry Maine* ISBN: *1-59462-128-4* **$29.95**
The chief object of the following pages is to indicate some of the earliest ideas of mankind, as they are reflected in Ancient Law, and to point out the relation of those ideas to modern thought. Religion/History Pages 452

Far-Away Stories *by William J. Locke* ISBN: *1-59462-129-2* **$19.45**
"Good wine needs no bush,' but a collection of mixed vintages does. And this book is just such a collection. Some of the stories I do not want to remain buried for ever in the museum files of dead magazine-numbers an author's not unpardonable vanity..." Fiction Pages 272

Life of David Crockett *by David Crockett* ISBN: *1-59462-250-7* **$27.45**
"Colonel David Crockett was one of the most remarkable men of the times in which he lived. Born in humble life, but gifted with a strong will, an indomitable courage, and unremitting perseverance,... Biographies/New Age Pages 424

Lip-Reading *by Edward Nitchie* ISBN: *1-59462-206-X* **$25.95**
Edward B. Nitchie, founder of the New York School for the Hard of Hearing, now the Nitchie School of Lip-Reading, Inc, wrote "LIP-READING Principles and Practice". The development and perfecting of this meritorious work on lip-reading was an undertaking... How-to Pages 400

A Handbook of Suggestive Therapeutics, Applied Hypnotism, Psychic Science ISBN: *1-59462-214-0* **$24.95**
by Henry Munro Health/New Age/Health/Self-help Pages 376

A Doll's House: and Two Other Plays *by Henrik Ibsen* ISBN: *1-59462-112-8* **$19.95**
Henrik Ibsen created this classic when in revolutionary 1848 Rome. Introducing some striking concepts in playwriting for the realist genre, this play has been studied the world over. Fiction/Classics/Plays 308

The Light of Asia *by sir Edwin Arnold* ISBN: *1-59462-204-3* **$13.95**
In this poetic masterpiece, Edwin Arnold describes the life and teachings of Buddha. The man who was to become known as Buddha to the world was born as Prince Gautama of India but he rejected the worldly riches and abandoned the reigns of power when... Religion/History/Biographies Pages 170

The Complete Works of Guy de Maupassant *by Guy de Maupassant* ISBN: *1-59462-157-8* **$16.95**
"For days and days, nights and nights, I had dreamed of that first kiss which was to consecrate our engagement, and I knew not on what spot I should put my lips..." Fiction/Classics Pages 240

The Art of Cross-Examination *by Francis L. Wellman* ISBN: *1-59462-309-0* **$26.95**
Written by a renowned trial lawyer, Wellman imparts his experience and uses case studies to explain how to use psychology to extract desired information through questioning. How-to/Science/Reference Pages 408

Answered or Unanswered? *by Louisa Vaughan* ISBN: *1-59462-248-5* **$10.95**
Miracles of Faith in China Religion Pages 112

The Edinburgh Lectures on Mental Science (1909) *by Thomas* ISBN: *1-59462-008-3* **$11.95**
This book contains the substance of a course of lectures recently given by the writer in the Queen Street Hall, Edinburgh. Its purpose is to indicate the Natural Principles governing the relation between Mental Action and Material Conditions... New Age/Psychology Pages 148

Ayesha *by H. Rider Haggard* ISBN: *1-59462-301-5* **$24.95**
Verily and indeed it is the unexpected that happens! Probably if there was one person upon the earth from whom the Editor of this, and of a certain previous history, did not expect to hear again... Classics Pages 380

Ayala's Angel *by Anthony Trollope* ISBN: *1-59462-352-X* **$29.95**
The two girls were both pretty, but Lucy who was twenty-one who supposed to be simple and comparatively unattractive, whereas Ayala was credited, as her Bombwhat romantic name might show, with poetic charm and a taste for romance. Ayala when her father died was nineteen... Fiction Pages 484

The American Commonwealth *by James Bryce* ISBN: *1-59462-286-8* **$34.45**
An interpretation of American democratic political theory. It examines political mechanics and society from the perspective of Scotsman James Bryce Politics Pages 572

Stories of the Pilgrims *by Margaret P. Pumphrey* ISBN: *1-59462-116-0* **$17.95**
This book explores pilgrims religious oppression in England as well as their escape to Holland and eventual crossing to America on the Mayflower, and their early days in New England... History Pages 268

QTY

The Fasting Cure *by Sinclair Upton* ISBN: *1-59462-222-1* **$13.95**
In the Cosmopolitan Magazine for May, 1910, and in the Contemporary Review (London) for April, 1910, I published an article dealing with my experiences in fasting. I have written a great many magazine articles, but never one which attracted so much attention... New Age/Self Help/Health Pages 164

Hebrew Astrology *by Sepharial* ISBN: *1-59462-308-2* **$13.45**
In these days of advanced thinking it is a matter of common observation that we have left many of the old landmarks behind and that we are now pressing forward to greater heights and to a wider horizon than that which represented the mind-content of our progenitors... Astrology Pages 144

Thought Vibration or The Law of Attraction in the Thought World ISBN: *1-59462-127-6* **$12.95**
by William Walker Atkinson *Psychology/Religion Pages 144*

Optimism *by Helen Keller* ISBN: *1-59462-108-X* **$15.95**
Helen Keller was blind, deaf, and mute since 19 months old, yet famously learned how to overcome these handicaps, communicate with the world, and spread her lectures promoting optimism. An inspiring read for everyone... Biographies/Inspirational Pages 84

Sara Crewe *by Frances Burnett* ISBN: *1-59462-360-0* **$9.45**
In the first place, Miss Minchin lived in London. Her home was a large, dull, tall one, in a large, dull square, where all the houses were alike, and all the sparrows were alike, and where all the door-knockers made the same heavy sound... Childrens/Classic Pages 88

The Autobiography of Benjamin Franklin *by Benjamin Franklin* ISBN: *1-59462-135-7* **$24.95**
The Autobiography of Benjamin Franklin has probably been more extensively read than any other American historical work, and no other book of its kind has had such ups and downs of fortune. Franklin lived for many years in England, where he was agent... Biographies/History Pages 332

Name	
Email	
Telephone	
Address	
City, State ZIP	

☐ **Credit Card**   ☐ **Check / Money Order**

Credit Card Number	
Expiration Date	
Signature	

Please Mail to: Book Jungle
PO Box 2226
Champaign, IL 61825
or Fax to: 630-214-0564

ORDERING INFORMATION

web: *www.bookjungle.com*
email: *sales@bookjungle.com*
fax: *630-214-0564*
mail: *Book Jungle PO Box 2226 Champaign, IL 61825*
or PayPal *to sales@bookjungle.com*

Please contact us for bulk discounts

DIRECT-ORDER TERMS

**20% Discount if You Order
Two or More Books**
Free Domestic Shipping!
Accepted: Master Card, Visa,
Discover, American Express

www.ingramcontent.com/pod-product-compliance
Lightning Source LLC
Chambersburg PA
CBHW081158170626
46813CB00009B/3238